ONTARIO GHOST STORIES

Volume II

D0711352

Barbara Smith

Ghost House Books

The Publisher: Ghost House Books
Distributed by Lone Pine Publishing
10145 – 81 Avenue
Edmonton, AB T6E 1W9
Canada

Website: http://www.ghostbooks.net

National Library of Canada Cataloguing in Publication Data
Smith, Barbara, 1947–
    Ontario ghost stories, vol. II

    ISBN 1-894877-14-4

    1. Ghosts—Ontario. 2. Legends—Ontario. I. Title.
GR113.5.O5S64 2002   398.2'0971305   C2002-910782-2

Editorial Director: Nancy Foulds
Project Editor: Shelagh Kubish
Editorial: Shelagh Kubish, Denise Dykstra, Randy Williams
Production Coordinator: Jennifer Fafard
Book Design, Layout & Production: Jeff Fedorkiw
Cover Design: Gerry Dotto

Photo Credits: Every effort has been made to accurately credit photographers. Any errors
or omissions should be directed to the publisher for changes in future editions. The
photographs in this book are reproduced with the kind permission of the following
sources: Stacey Kew (p. 16, 17); Robert Mowers (p. 60, 66); Barbara Smith (p. 77, 123, 144,
197); anonymous contributor (p. 80, 81); Dennis Smyk (p. 95); Kate Geisler (p. 164).

The stories, folklore and legends in this book are based on the author's research of sources
including individuals whose experiences have led them to believe they have encountered
phenomena of some kind or another. They are meant to entertain, and neither the publisher nor the authors claim these stories represent fact.

We acknowledge the financial support of the Government of Canada through the Book
Publishing Industry Development Program (BPIDP) for our publishing activities.

PC: P5

Dedication

For Bob, with love

Contents

Chapter Four: Haunted Institutions

Chapter Five: They Returned

Chapter Six: The Spirit's Inn

Acknowledgements

This book is the result of a great deal of effort from many people, but everyone's efforts would have been in vain if it were not for the management and staff at Ghost House Books. My gratitude to each one of you for the important role you play in making these books a reality. I owe a special thank-you to Grant Kennedy, Shane Kennedy, Nancy Foulds, Shelagh Kubish, Denise Dykstra, Randy Williams and Jeff Fedorkiw. Please know that I do deeply appreciate all your efforts on my behalf.

Many others have also contributed in various ways to the realization of this volume. Steve Bartlett first contacted me when I was writing *Ontario Ghost Stories* (Lone Pine Publishing, 1998). Since then Steve and I have remained in friendly and supportive contact with one another. Steve was an enormous help with this book, too. Thank you.

W. Ritchie Benedict is the most tenacious researcher and reliable correspondent I've ever had the pleasure of knowing. Many thanks, Ritchie, for all your input over the years!

Kate Geisler and I were in touch several years ago when *Ontario Ghost Stories* came out. When I contacted Kate about this book, I had no idea just how well the reconnection between the two of us would work. Kate very kindly and generously shared local ghost stories that she'd collected over the years. As a wonderful but completely unexpected bonus, Kate and I became friends during our e-mail exchanges to clarify details of one encounter or another. It's been great, Kate. Thank you. I look forward to helping you tackle a book-length project sometime in the near future.

I would also like to thank Greg Carter, Claire Gigantes, Hugh Francisci, Ron Gostlin, Emerson Haneman, Fran Hanover,

Stacey Kew, Robert Mowers, Judy and Heinz Puersten, Laura Ristau, Kim Roddick, Samantha Bigley, Dennis Smyck, Sharon Tapp and Cheryl Vardon. Some contributors have requested anonymity. I understand and respect that decision. Please accept my gratitude and public acknowledgement; this book would not have been nearly as much fun to compile and write without your contributions. (All correct names and pertinent documentation are held in the author's files.)

Thank you to the Edmonton Public Library staff, especially those at Idylwylde Branch and the Interlibrary Loan Department.

In addition, I would like to pay special tribute to the people closest to me and to thank them for their support in all areas of my life. Without them I could not even think of taking on projects such as my books. These people are my husband, Bob, my daughters, Debbie and Robyn, as well as my two closest friends and fellow authors, Jo-Anne Christensen and Dr. Barrie Robinson. I love you and I thank you for your enormous contributions to my life and to my work.

Introduction

When I finished writing *Ontario Ghost Stories* (Lone Pine Publishing, 1998), I was convinced that I'd never again have such a good time collecting and writing true ghost stories. I was wrong. Compiling this volume was an even more gratifying experience. The people with whom I've come into contact while working on *Ontario Ghost Stories, Volume II* have been as varied and intriguing as the stories those people so generously shared with me.

Such variation, though, can lead to a story style that is different than those neat and tidy tales to which we have grown accustomed. Where is the beginning? Is there a nice long middle section? And how about the ending? Surely, all the loose ends will be tied up succinctly by the final sentence. We are used to that type of structure in our reading material. But that perfect symmetry only works for fiction. The stories in this book are descriptions of actual events. No one has made them up. Quite to the contrary, people have lived and are living them—and as we all know, real lives are rarely made up of well-arranged events. So it is then with these narratives, for these are all "true" ghost stories.

I put the word "true" in quotation marks because while I believe in the concept of ghosts, I am also open to the possibility that such occurrences may be something else entirely. There are many legitimate questions surrounding the notion of phantoms. For instance, are ghosts external or internal to those who encounter them? It would seem that there is not one correct answer to that question. Hauntings are unique and, as such, might each be caused by a unique set of circumstances.

As an example, when a person sees an apparition, has that manifestation popped into the reality of the witness or has the observer stepped into a ghost's time and place? Again, I don't believe that a blanket explanation can suffice. It might be that during those moments of special sightings we are in a time loop, or perhaps we are just occasionally aware of that which we do not normally acknowledge. To my mind, this lack of consistency does not make the experience—or the ghost—any less real.

And there are many other fascinating possibilities to ponder. For example, Steve Bartlett, an Ontario-based geological engineer, suggests that events which have a profound impact on our lives may leave imprints upon our aural (or psychic) energy fields. Perhaps ghosts are merely activations of those aural archives. Dramatic events, especially death, will crystallize psychic energy so that "instead of flowing, like a hot liquid, [the energy] will undergo a forced change." This change, according to Bartlett's reasoned conjecture, could freeze or set in place energy-causing manifestations beyond that which we can normally sense. In some instances we have chosen to call the manifestations of these sensations "ghosts."

Whether Steve Bartlett's theory is the correct one or not, it is certainly thought provoking. Whatever the eventual explanation for a ghostly encounter may be, I am convinced that such events are a profoundly effecting part of the human experience.

A very convincing incident in support of the premise that ghosts do exist occurred while I was writing this book. A resident of the Ottawa area wrote to me offering details of unexplained events that occurred in her home. The story was frankly quite frightening, but my correspondent seemed to take consolation from the fact that all the horrors had taken place some years ago and only after a particular incident. Besides, the house had been "cleansed" by a member of the clergy after the haunting. I replied to the woman, expressing my gratitude to her for having shared such personal specifics for publication in this book.

Several weeks later, I received another message from the lady. This time she requested that I pull the story from inclusion in the book. Apparently the horrible haunting had returned. From the day she sent that first note to me, inexplicable and unpleasant events had once again begun occurring in the family's home. These were not instances that could be overlooked or "lived with"; this paranormal recurrence was so bad on one particular night that the members of the household were forced to flee from their home. It was clear, the woman wrote, that the ghost did not want its chronicle made public. I immediately deleted the contribution from my computer files. I sincerely hope that the force we disturbed with our written discussion has somehow calmed down again by now. To this family I wish respectful "peace to all."

Happily, the vast majority of true ghost tales are positive ones. I hope you will enjoy reading this collection of Ontario ghost stories as much as I have enjoyed writing them. Please keep in mind that I am not a paranormal expert by any means. I am merely a storyteller with a special affection for the combination of history and mystery. Now I invite you to turn down the lights, read on and enjoy a very different trip through Ontario's geography, past and present.

1
Haunted Houses

∽

Be they ever so humble, we all love our homes.
We love the familiarity, security and comfort they
provide—and, for some of us, the haunting experiences.

∽

Promises Kept

The rate at which word spreads when I'm collecting material for a new book in this series is nothing short of astonishing. Perhaps it's even supernatural. People who love true ghost stories must be linked into a communications grapevine of sorts. Shortly after I began gathering information for this volume, dozens of folks with Ontario-based stories to tell came forward and kindly offered to share their tales with me.

Stacey Kew is one of those people. I am deeply grateful to Stacey for having taken time out of her busy life to let me know about her paranormal experiences. Happily, she is equally appreciative of the opportunity to recount those experiences because Jimmy, her friend from the afterlife, made two requests of her and she agreed to fulfill them both. Stacey had no idea how she was going to honour those commitments; she only knew that she would. It is a privilege to be a part of this earth-to-beyond pact. I present the story to you as Stacey related it to me.

The young woman began the tale of her supernatural experiences by explaining that all the ghost of Jimmy ever desired was acknowledgement. "That's why he contacted me," she wrote. "All he wanted was to let someone know the truth about his death." Then Stacey set the events of the narrative into context. The occurrences started in the spring of 1997, in the Toronto suburb of Scarborough—a place that is far different today than it was when Jimmy lived and died there.

"I was asleep after work one day," Stacey described. "It was just starting to get dark outside. I woke up and saw someone standing at the foot of my bed. Assuming it was

Bruce, my husband, I asked him what he was doing home so much earlier than usual and then I fell back asleep. Later, when I got up and asked my husband what time he had come home, he said that he had just arrived."

Stacey was a bit unnerved by her husband's reply because she felt sure that she'd seen him much earlier. Bruce just thought his wife had been dreaming. But the man was not able to stick with his dismissive attitude for long because other strange incidents soon began to occur.

"A few weeks later, my husband was asleep at dusk and he woke up to see someone at the foot of the bed. He assumed it was me and fell back asleep. When I came home several hours later, he asked me what I had come home for earlier," Stacey continued. "A short while later, we were sitting in the kitchen eating lunch and I looked over at Bruce. He had lost all the colour in his face. He told me that someone had just walked upstairs. I got up from the table and had a look but could see nothing."

The number of strange occurrences was quickly growing, but at the time Stacey responded in perhaps the only way she could—by simply getting on with things. Much to her surprise, as she carried on with the everyday missions in her life, the ghost carried on with those in his afterlife.

"Later, I was sitting in the living room watching television. Worf, one of my cats, was sound asleep on a dining room chair when he suddenly bolted across the dining room into the living room and bounced off the window. He jumped back on to the ledge and his hair was standing on end. He was hunched, wide-eyed and his tail was about four times its normal size."

Stacey was so startled by the animal's sudden flight that at first all she could do was stare at him. But after taking a second to calm herself, she had the clarity to extend her focus. "I followed [Worf's] gaze and discovered a man standing in the doorway to the dining room. He didn't have any definite features. He looked like someone had blown smoke into the form of a man. I did know that he was a man, though, and that he was tall and wearing a trench coat."

Stacey said she was "freaked out" by this vision because she was "wide awake and completely coherent." She couldn't dismiss the sighting as a dream. Besides, she had physical proof that something out of the ordinary had just taken place: her cat had been injured in his full-speed collision with the living room window.

"I had to take my cat to work with me the next day (I work in a veterinarian's clinic) because Worf was still sore and needed to be examined. I think I am one of the few people who has the following written in her cat's file: 'Saw a ghost last night and panicked. Collided with the window. Is bruised and anxious. Needs rest.' "

By now Stacey was almost certain that something very strange was at work in her house. Any remaining doubts faded early one morning when she was in bed reading. "It was about 2 AM and I heard a scratching or squeaking noise coming from my closet," she wrote. "I shone the light towards the closet but couldn't see anything.

"My dog was looking at the closet and growling. My arms began to get covered in goosebumps. Then the squeaking noise started again. I looked up to see a pants hanger with about four pairs of pants on it start to move across the clothes closet rod. I panicked. The hanger was fairly heavy and I could hear it skipping as it moved. It probably moved a few inches and then moved back."

Several ghosts remained in the house this boy lived in...

At that point Stacey's tolerance level had reached its limit. "I lost it!" she confessed. "I got out of that room so quickly. I ran around the house turning every light on, but not before grabbing my teddy bear and a pair of scissors—what else are you going to use to defend yourself against the unseen? When my husband arrived home from work at 3:30 AM, he found me rocking back and forth on the couch repeating murmuring, 'Oh, my God. Oh, my God.' "

The woman was endlessly relieved to have another human being in the house with her. "I don't think I have been more afraid in my life than I was that night," she declared. "It was at that point that I decided to have [a psychic] come to the house and find out who was here and what he wanted."

...did one of them show up in this photo?

Stacey contacted a psychic named Dave, who came to the home with two other psychics. They started their work in the bedroom because that was where the majority of the activity had taken place. Almost immediately, all three of the psychics picked up on something. That in itself was not unusual; what was strange was that each of them sensed a different presence.

One psychic intuited "a boy with orange hair and freckles." That pleasant image was ruined by the fact that the boy was "covered in blood." Another member of the group got a mental picture of the same boy, but a large dog was with him. The third detected the presence of "a priest, a tall man in an overcoat," as well as "another, quite nasty presence that wasn't there all the time."

The clairvoyants determined that the boy's name was James Albert Evans and that he was 12 years old. They explained to Stacey that the spirit of this child had moved the pants hanger. They believed the action was not meant to be frightening.

"He just wanted my attention—and he got it!" Stacey exclaimed. "All he wanted was to let someone know the truth about his death. He was murdered with an axe by his mentally ill father. The murder was covered up by a priest (the nasty figure in the overcoat) because Jimmy's father was considered an important member of the community and the church. I was absolutely amazed and stunned by what I heard, and I made a promise to help Jimmy get his story told."

Stacey readily acknowledged that her experience that day was completely different from anything she had ever encountered before. "I couldn't believe I was a part of the events that were unfolding," she wrote. "Had someone told me this story, I don't think I would have believed them. But this was all going on right in front of my eyes."

The young woman and the psychics moved into the living room. A few minutes later, Stacey felt the hair on her arms and neck stand up. "I said, 'He's in the room with us, isn't he?' The psychics told me he was standing behind me."

Stacey spent the entire afternoon with her ghostly housemate and the three people who could communicate with him. She called it an amazing experience. "Jimmy's ghost sat on the floor in the living room with us, singing nursery rhymes," she wrote. "Jimmy told us about things in the house that the psychics could not have otherwise known."

It turns out that Jimmy had been startled by the noise and confusion that resulted when Stacey and her husband began renovating the basement of the house he'd secretly been sharing with them. The resident wraith even had an opinion about the tenant who eventually rented the suite that had been constructed.

Jimmy stated that he "didn't like the man who lived downstairs because he yelled a lot and it scared him." To retaliate, the entity "would play tricks by knocking on the apartment door." Stacey remembered that her tenant used to complain about the distinct and frequent banging sounds on the entranceway to the suite.

According to Stacey, Jimmy also explained some of his personal history. "He said he was attached to the property, not to the house," she wrote. "His grandfather had owned a farm that included what was now our property. Jimmy used to play in the corner of my yard."

Stacey and the three psychics were then invited to take a ghostly stroll down Jimmy's memory lane. "He wanted us to go outside, so we did," Stacey wrote. "He told us how upset he had been when a particular tree was removed. It was a very large tree that had been removed the previous year because the roots were damaging the foundation of the house. Because the grass had since grown over that spot, there was no evidence for the psychics to see that anything had ever been there but lawn. Jimmy told us about a river that flowed through his grandfather's property and behind my property line."

Having been treated to a trip through the history of "her" property, Stacey was rather surprised to learn why the ghost had chosen her to communicate with. "He was attracted to me in particular because I had a little girl spirit with me who made Jimmy feel safe and because he felt that I would respond," she explained.

The reason the phantom wanted to communicate was simple: "All he wanted was to have someone to know the truth. He had two requests of me—that I make his story known and that I find his grave."

The young woman began her attempt to satisfy the first part of Jimmy's request by relating her incredible experience to anyone who would listen. She included the spirit's description of the spot in which his body had been buried. Through the psychics, Jimmy had "described his grave as a mossy place under a tree and beside a larger grave that looked like his. That other burial plot was his mother's."

Stacey spent many hours in the library and in local cemeteries. "I discovered a James Albert Evans who had died in 1912, but no information about the cause of death or where he was buried," she wrote. "Next I found a map of the area from 1900. It showed the divisions of land and the names of the various landowners. Our property did in fact lie within the boundaries of his grandfather's farm, and there was a river that ran behind my property line."

Despite her intensive research, Stacey was unsuccessful at finding Jimmy's grave. "I became very frustrated," she admitted, "because it is hard to ask questions with limited information from a ghost. People just aren't receptive under those conditions. I decided there had to be a way to communicate directly with Jimmy, so I put magnetic letters and numbers on the fridge. I didn't know if it would work, but I was willing to try anything."

One day, after a particularly frustrating phone call with a man from the historical society, Stacey came home and said out loud, "I'm really trying here, but you've got to help me out." The next morning she looked at the magnets on the fridge and, much to her surprise, the letter *B* and the numbers *1* and *2* had been separated from the rest. A breakthrough! "Except I had no idea what *B12* referred to," Stacey admitted. "I didn't care too much, though. I was just so happy to have found a way to communicate with Jimmy. It was a wonderful experience."

Stacey continued, "Life carried on, but my efforts to find Jimmy's grave were never rewarded. Then came August 12, 1997, a sad day that I will never forget. I received a phone call from one of the psychics who had connected with Jimmy when she was in the house. She told me that she had 'sent Jimmy on.' "

Stacey's reaction to losing her supernatural friend was as dramatic as when she first realized her house was haunted: "I was crushed. I couldn't understand why she had sent him on. I was angry and I still wanted him. What upset me the most was that I never said goodbye to him."

As Stacey reacted to this devastating news, she became aware of the depth of her feelings for Jimmy. "I was quite surprised by my reaction," she wrote. "I actually cried. It seemed ridiculous to be so upset but he had become a part of my life and my heart. Jimmy did have a final message for me, though. He thanked me and asked me to continue to look for his grave. He also told me not to worry because he would forever protect me from negative energies."

Stacey's resolve to solve the puzzle was renewed. Unfortunately, it only lasted a short while. "I promised myself that I would never stop looking, but life has a way of getting in the way," she explained. "I never did forget Jimmy, or the promise I had made, but I resigned myself to never finding his grave and I did stop actively looking."

But the paranormal world had one more surprise waiting for its earthly friend. "There was this one cemetery that I kept going to, but the gate was always locked and I had no idea how to find out anything about the place," Stacey recalled. "A couple of years after Jimmy left, my neighbour Liz called me to find out what cemetery I had not been able to get into."

Stacey described in vivid detail the location of the one unexplored graveyard. "This is where the story gets weird," Stacey wrote. The "weirdness" came in the form of a key to the cemetery in question. Stacey's neighbour had somehow come into possession of the only way to unlock the gate.

"I'm not sure how, but sometimes it's best not to ask," Stacey declared before continuing with her tale. "The following week, I met my neighbour at the cemetery and we found Jimmy's grave. It was under a tree, beside a similar but larger stone. It was in a mossy area." And just as Jimmy had indicated, "it was in the second row (B) and it was the 12th grave from the left."

As soon as Stacey touched the tombstone, she felt the hair on her arms stand on end. "I was covered with goosebumps," she recalled. "It was amazing. The code on the fridge finally made sense. I had fulfilled that promise I made to Jimmy."

The amazing story of Stacey and Jimmy has an equally astonishing postscript. "Every year I hang a Christmas stocking for Jimmy and I think of him a lot," the young woman wrote. "He became a very special member of my household, and I will be forever grateful for having been chosen by him to experience what I did. Although I never knew him in life, he made his way into my heart and is very special to me. He really was a sweet little boy."

At this point it would have been safe to assume that Stacey's adventures beyond the physical world were over. But that was not the case. "Jimmy's presence seemed to be a door opener of sorts," Stacey wrote, "because I have never been alone in the house since."

She added, "I love having the ghosts. I am not afraid of them because I understand more now. When they bug me, I tell them to stop and they do. That's more than I can say about my kids or my pets! Psychics love coming to my house because they never know what they are going to find. I have been told that the middle of March 2002 will bring more spirits into my house. I am waiting with my arms wide open because it is just far too quiet now!"

Without Jimmy's promise to protect her from negative energy, it is doubtful that Stacey would be quite so confident. Thankfully, both parties involved in the agreement that crossed time, space and human understanding have kept their side of the bargain to date. Stacey has not been discomfited by any of the manifestations that share her Scarborough home from time to time, and Jimmy's story has been shared with many. That audience now includes all of us.

And what of the prediction that Stacey would experience more visitations in March 2002? It seems to have been correct. Stacey recently informed me that she noticed a distinct change in the atmosphere of her house around that time—and she saw an apparition. But despite all she's been through with the spirit world, the haunting caught her off guard.

"Having been in a quiet house for so long, I'm embarrassed to admit that seeing the ghost scared me half to death," she said. "I was sitting on the couch vegetating and he appeared in the corner of the living room about 6 feet [approximately 2 metres] from me. It certainly got me out of my vegetative state pretty quick! I have also heard a voice a few times but can't be certain it was the voice of a spirit. I do have the feeling of not being alone anymore."

And so both life and afterlife continue in Stacey's haunted house.

Spirit on Sarah Street

Cheryl wrote a long, detailed letter to me describing her family's experiences while sharing their home with a ghost. During the years the Vardon family lived in the haunted house, Cheryl was very young and had her own name for the spirit. She called him the Yucky Man.

Cheryl's family consisted of herself, her parents and her two older brothers. In June 1982, the group moved to a house on Sarah Street in Gravenhurst, a town at the southern end of Lake Muskoka. At the time, they could not have guessed what a life-changing move this would be.

Others in the community might have been aware that there was something abnormal about their new house, but as Cheryl explained, "being new to the town, we had no idea what we were about to experience."

The first signs of the haunting were initially not given much thought. They seemed to be unusual incidences, yes, but quite isolated and certainly not the kind of activity that would lead most people to suspect there was a ghost in their midst. Hindsight, however, indicates that even then the presence was trying to make itself known.

The earliest occurrence was in the kitchen, where a pair of double-hung windows were sealed tightly shut. Cheryl's dad tried everything to open them, but nothing ever worked. Then one day Cheryl's mom walked into the room and found the windows wide open. The Vardons might have been grateful for the fresh air, but their appreciation was over-shadowed by confusion because, as Cheryl acknowledged, "Nobody in our family had opened them!"

A few weeks later, in keeping with a time-honoured Ontario custom, Cheryl, her mother and her brothers left to spend the summer at their cottage. Cheryl's father joined them there on weekends. During the week, he stayed in the city, and his Monday-to-Friday routine was often punctuated by loud footsteps coming up the stairs and then walking down the hall. It didn't take long for Mr. Vardon to realize that he was sharing the house with a ghost.

By the end of the summer, when the rest of the family moved back home, the spirit had become an accepted part of life on Sarah Street. Cheryl wrote, "I saw a man in my room many nights. He was standing at the end of my bed. I would scream, cry and yell. I was very young, but I told my parents what I saw and I referred to him as the Yucky Man. My parents tell me that I saw him a lot!"

This image could not have been a figment of Cheryl's imagination because Aaron, one of her brothers, also saw the apparition. "He told my mom that a man was coming up the back walkway," Cheryl wrote. "He described the man as wearing dirty trousers, a jacket and a cap. My mother went to the door and nobody was there." No one that she could see anyway.

No doubt the ghost Aaron and Cheryl saw was the same phantom that frequently interrupted the family's dinners.

When everyone was seated at the table eating supper, a particular door to the outside would open and close on its own. This disturbance became so routine, Cheryl recalled, "that my parents just joked about it, telling the phantom to come on in and sit down for dinner."

The sense of a presence was stronger in some parts of the house than in others. For example, Cheryl noted that "my mother would always get a shiver up her spine as she reached the second stair from the top when she was walking upstairs. She still does not know why."

The poor woman likely could have put up with the temporary cases of the shivers if the ghost would only have left her glasses alone! Mrs. Vardon would frequently discover that her reading glasses had been mangled and broken for no apparent reason.

Another area with an unappealing aura was the main washroom. "I hated using it," Cheryl said. "I preferred to go all the way down to the unfinished basement and use the toilet in the wide open room." That certainly seems like a strange choice for a little girl to make, but it makes sense if one believes Cheryl's mother's theory. Mrs. Vardon thought it possible that in life the spirit had been responsible for the litter of cigarette burns in the washroom, and that he retained a proprietary interest in the lavatory after death.

After a time, there was no denying that the house was haunted. Cheryl's parents needed help and information. They talked to a friend named Irene who was knowledgeable about the paranormal. Irene began doing some research. "We found out that the Yucky Man had lived in the house years ago," Cheryl wrote. "He was a mechanic who had a car business. His name was Dint Green and he lived in the house with his wife."

Mrs. Green died, but Mr. Green stayed on in the house except for his winter vacations in Arizona. Tragically, he was killed in a fire during one of those stays in the warmer climate. From the Vardons' experiences, it was clear that the man's soul had returned to "his" home in Gravenhurst. And judging by the back door opening and closing, it was evident that the spirit was keeping to his lifelong routine of coming in regularly at suppertime.

After retrieving the information on the Greens, Irene carried her investigation even farther. "She contacted the family who had lived in the house before us," Cheryl continued. "Apparently Dint's presence had been the reason they moved. They told Irene that one of their children had been pushed down the stairs by an unseen force. Another child woke up with teeth marks in her back."

Digging farther into the history of the home's ownership proved fruitless. As Cheryl wrote, "The couple who lived in the house before that family would not even discuss it!"

Irene's advice to the Vardons was straightforward. She believed the ghost in their house was "an evil spirit," and she recommended that they either move at once or call an exorcist. Mr. and Mrs. Vardon decided not to do either. They resolved that if anyone was hurt, they'd react, but otherwise they'd ignore the entity as best they could. Cheryl was far too young to have had a say in this decision, but she does reflect nearly 20 years later that she still thinks "he scared me too much to have wanted to stay."

The Vardons' lack of action ultimately proved to be wise. "One day, my mother did not get the chills on the second stair and I stopped seeing the Yucky Man," Cheryl said. "We figured that the ghost had left."

Cheryl's family moved out of the house two years later. When they sold the place, they paid the purchasers the courtesy of informing them that the home had been haunted. By coincidence, the new owner was a teacher at the elementary school Cheryl attended. The girl often asked the woman if Mr. Green had been back. She always said no.

"Who knows," my correspondent mused. "Maybe Dint finally found his way to his wife."

Ghostly Guardian

Although I have altered Leila Campbell's name slightly to protect her anonymity, the following story is told as the woman herself detailed it—nearly 50 years ago in *FATE* magazine.

On a dark and stormy night in 1929, Leila, less than five years old at the time, lay sleeping in her Hamilton home when the sounds of the tempest awakened her. The little girl had long been frightened of violent weather and usually called out for her parents to come to her room during a storm. On this particular evening, however, she was calm and unafraid. You see, little Leila knew with great certainty that she was not alone in her bedroom. She also knew that the person with her would protect her from any possible harm.

Moments after waking, Leila realized that her bedroom was filled with the "faint aroma of damp heather and newly mowed hay." Pleasant fragrances, yes, but decidedly strange ones for someone to encounter in an urban southern Ontario setting. Then she began to see an image forming in the air before her eyes.

The figure became more and more distinct as the fascinated child watched, until finally the girl was able to discern that her unexpected but most intriguing visitor was an elderly lady with snow white hair and "deep-set blue eyes." This encounter was, it turned out, the first of many such visitations that Leila would receive from beyond the grave.

Over the course of the following year, Leila saw the ethereal woman frequently. On one of those occasions, perhaps as a gesture of comfort, the reassuring wraith even reached out and grasped the child's small, warm hand within her cold, ghostly one.

Because she was completely comfortable with the spirit's presence, it was a long time before the little girl mentioned her new friend to an adult. But one day, when Leila and her beloved grandfather, William MacFarland Campbell, were alone together, she shared her secret. Many years later, she could still vividly recall the older man's "startled" reaction to her description of this very special visitor.

The older man told his granddaughter that although he had never been blessed by an encounter with a spirit, he had always been intensely interested in the "world beyond." Campbell relished hearing Leila's revelations about the apparition and responded by telling her legendary supernatural tales from their ancestral home of Inversaid in Scotland.

Less than 10 years later, Leila's grandfather died. The girl was given a keepsake as a reminder of the man and her close relationship with him—a gold key that Mr. Campbell had always worn on the chain of his pocket watch.

As Leila grew to maturity she developed a habit of gently rubbing the treasured artifact. This unintentional polishing soon revealed that someone, many years earlier, had inscribed a single word on the key: "Inversaid." Oddly, this discovery actually changed the things the youngster was able to see during her nighttime visits from the ghost. Now Leila saw not only the spirit herself but also thatched cottages, heather and bog myrtle.

To confirm the nocturnal sightings that she knew to be very real, Leila would occasionally mention her experiences to other adults in her life. Sadly, she never again received anything like the positive reaction that her grandfather had shown her. Instead, these other people belittled her encounters as fantasy tales and urged her to become more responsible and adult-like. Leila conformed to their wishes; as she did, her visitor came to see her less and less often. Finally, at some point in Leila's teen years, the girl was left with only the memories of the wonderful experiences lodged in the deepest recesses of her mind.

And that is where those fond memories might have remained if it hadn't been for a phone call Leila Campbell received in the early 1960s. She was, of course, an adult by then and had been living in Spokane, Washington, for some years. The passage of time made a call from a clerk at Rawlinsons Limited, a storage company in Toronto, even more surprising.

Leila's great-aunt, just recently deceased, had left a steamer trunk at the Rawlinsons warehouse with Leila's name and address as a reference. If Leila would pay for the storage fees and the shipping costs, someone at the company would be happy to send the trunk to her. Understandably curious, Leila arranged to have the potential treasure chest shipped west. One month later, a very old container arrived at her home.

Opening the ancient piece of luggage was a simple matter because its locks had completely deteriorated. Strong musty odours of camphor, mothballs and just plain age mingled together and assaulted Leila's nose as she raised the trunk's lid. An assortment of ladies shoes, hand-made dresses, cleverly created purses and even a crocheted stole lay before her eyes. Carefully removing each article and setting it aside, the woman found more and more treasures with every layer she unpacked.

Way down in the bottom of the trunk, wrapped in an aging quilt, Leila found something very strange—a smaller trunk. Was this perhaps a puzzle within a puzzle? No, this revelation turned out to be a key of sorts to unlocking an almost lifelong mystery. The lock on this smaller trunk had not worn with age. It held tight. But Leila was not concerned, because she knew with complete, almost child-like certainty that she had the key to open this second piece of luggage. It was the key she had kept to remember her grandfather by.

Leila inserted and turned the small gold keepsake. As she had known in her soul it would, the clasp released and the lid opened. Instantly, the fragrances of heather and newly mowed hay wafted up to envelope Leila in a reverie of memory. She was shocked to find a photograph beneath the stash of books, table linens and parchments. It was an old photo, but Leila had no trouble identifying the figure in it as the spirit who had come to visit her so many times during her childhood.

On the back of the photo was written the subject's name and the date on which the picture had been taken. The ghost who had offered comfort to a little girl growing up in Ontario was the spirit of her great-grandmother—Leila's dearly loved grandfather's mother.

Not only had the long-deceased woman been able to create a memory of herself for Leila Campbell, she had also found a way to pass along some of her own beautifully made and well-preserved handicrafts. Once again, the revenant with the deep-set blue eyes and snow white hair had been able to pay her beloved great-granddaughter a visit—from years and miles beyond the grave.

A Grave Story

Being raised in a home just metres from a haunted house has understandably left a lasting impression on Emerson Haneman.

Haneman, a delightful gentleman who now lives in Port Stanley, Ontario, was brought up on a farm near the outskirts of Ottawa. The property consisted of two houses, a small graveyard and the usual farm buildings. It was the neighbouring residence that contained a ghost.

"Back in the mid-'30s we lived with that haunted house in the next field to us," Haneman recalled, adding that the amount of strange activity in the dwelling left little room for disbelief. "No one lived there, yet we would see up-to-date newspapers in the home and dishes on the table that changed every time we went into the house or even looked in the windows."

Young Emerson and his family were not the only ones to notice the supernatural occurrences in the residence. Other neighbours reported that on certain nights there would be lamps lit in the abandoned building.

Even more frequently, ghostly cries were said to be heard emanating from the place. "As youngsters, we would shake in our beds at night whenever we heard those screams," Haneman said.

There didn't seem to be much question as to whose spirit inhabited the dwelling. "The laneway [leading to that home] is where a witch was supposed to have be burnt at the stake," Haneman explained. "They say it was her ghost that haunted the house next to ours."

Mr. Haneman also recalled that small children were buried in the graveyard on the property. Because the occupants of those tiny graves were no doubt emotionally linked to the farm, and because the abandoned residence adjacent to the Hanemans' house was haunted, it's tempting to assume that there is some sort of connection between the graves and the haunting spirits. But in this case, such an association is unlikely. The presence of those graves probably just contributed to the general otherworldly atmosphere of the place.

Farmhouse Phantom

Fran Hanover was only eight years old when her parents bought a farm on Alsace Road in the Township of Nipissing, southwest of North Bay. At that time, her friend Kate Geisler, who related this true ghost tale to me, already held her in extremely high regard.

"It never ceases to amaze me," Kate wrote, "that people whom you've known for years will sometimes suddenly let you inside their own little memory bank of private stories. Such was the case with Fran, probably the most incredible person I have ever met. She's smart, witty and charming, and her hearty laugh is matched only by her zest for life and a good story. And she had one."

Fran's parents immigrated to Canada from Germany. They settled in Toronto, where they adopted Fran, and then in 1977 purchased and moved to the farm where this story takes place. Fran found country living quiet compared to what she'd known in the city. But that opinion held only "until the ghosts arrived."

Kate described the haunted house as being "like most farm homes in the area—a three-storey wood home with white aluminum, brick-shaped siding with a wraparound porch, an attached wood shed and a tiny widow's walk. There seemed to be nothing unusual, nothing creepy about it."

But appearances, as we all know, can be deceiving. Neighbours let Fran's parents know that the place had something of a dramatic history. The house they purchased was actually the fifth residence to stand on its 165-year-old foundation. The previous four incarnations had all burned to the ground.

Other than that, Kate assured me, nothing seemed strange about the dwelling. "Nothing at all," she wrote. "Not at first anyway…All seemed well with the family's new home, right up to the night that sounds of footsteps were heard walking around on the downstairs floor."

The first time she heard the footfalls, Fran's mother got out of bed to discipline a mischievous child or two. Much to her surprise, she found that the area where she had heard the noises was completely empty. Since there wasn't any reason for her to be up, the woman returned to her bed. As soon as she did, the sounds of footsteps started up again.

Kate explained that the tired farmwife "stormed downstairs [a second time] and, being fearful of little in life, shouted to whomever was making this noise to stop as it was keeping her family and herself awake. That outburst proved successful, for no other footsteps were heard after that."

The haunting was far from over, though, because by this time Fran had noticed that "there was one bedroom on the top floor that was always uncomfortable to sleep in. She never wanted to stay in that room overnight. Unfortunately, it was *her* bedroom."

It's unlikely that the youngster's discomfort was merely a figment of her imagination. The girl's bedroom, Kate explained, was directly above "the parlour—the same part of the house where funerals had been held many years earlier. And the parlour was directly above the section of the basement that everyone in the family seemed to avoid without question."

It wasn't long before Fran began to have bad dreams. "These dreams had something of an uncommon twist to them," Kate recalled. "Fran firmly believed that they were caused, at least in part, by her bedroom itself. She remembers that as the frequency of these dreams increased, they became rather horrific nightmares of an angry woman chasing her throughout the upper floor of the house. The dream terrors became so vivid and increasingly terrifying that Fran's dreamland escapes from the phantom woman crossed over to reality and led to dangerous sleepwalking activities."

Fortunately, another supernatural force was also at work in the house. Fran's mother claimed that on the nights her daughter would sleepwalk, "some sort of alarm would go off in her mind. It was like a voice telling her that something serious was happening in the house. She would check throughout the house and inevitably find Fran missing from her room.

"This sixth sense awakened Mrs. Hanover a number of times," Kate continued. "The most terrifying episode took place during one of the coldest nights of the year when Fran's mother discovered her daughter down the hall. She was in a spare bedroom, sound asleep on a mattress that had no blankets or pillows. Worse, that room was unheated. It was so incredibly cold in the room that Fran's mother could see her breath."

The woman was badly shaken, but she was also very grateful that she had been able to find Fran before any harm had come to the child. Unfortunately, the situation was about to reveal itself as being even more bizarre than it first seemed. When Mrs. Hanover put her hand on her daughter, she realized that even though the room was so cold, Fran's body was warm to the touch. The little girl should have been hypothermic.

Kate revealed that Fran's mother was so distressed by the incident that she "told the story only once, then refused to speak of it ever again." Perhaps the scare involving one of her children was more than she could bear, for the woman was willing to speak freely about visits she herself received from the resident house-haunter.

One day, while she was doing laundry, Fran's mother got a little help from beyond the grave. Kate explained: "As was the norm with houses such as this one, there were doors at the end of the staircases so that the upper floor could be closed off during winter to conserve heat. Fran recalled that in this house the hinges on the door to the staircase from the main floor were worn. This wear and tear, combined with a slightly slanted floor, meant that the door to the staircase would not stay ajar unless it was blocked open."

Mrs. Hanover had not propped the door open, so when she reached the stairs, the entranceway was firmly closed. The woman stopped short, wondering how in the world she was going to juggle her awkward load and turn the doorknob at the same time. She needn't have worried. "Mumbling under her breath, with her arms full, Fran's mother watched in amazement as the door handle slowly turned and the door opened—all of its own accord."

This small act of kindness was neither the last nor the most important that the ghost would perform for the family. Very late one night, Fran's mother was awakened once again by the sounds of footsteps downstairs. Again she thought that her children had slipped from their beds and were up wandering about the house when they should have been sleeping.

Fran's mother was about to start down the stairs to retrieve her wayward offspring when a voice behind her clearly instructed, "Don't go down there!" She immediately whirled around, but no one was there. As the understandably confused woman turned back to look down the stairs, she was horrified to see "two very real men with very real guns robbing the family's home."

If it hadn't been for the phantom voice speaking its warning, Mrs. Hanover would have gone downstairs and, no doubt, startled the burglars. The likely consequences of her interruption were something too unbearable to think about.

Kate concluded the story of Fran's haunted house by relating what was perhaps the most prolonged ghostly session that occurred. These bizarre events happened when Fran's older sister, Gudrun, came for a visit. "Gudrun is one of those highly sensitive people who can feel and sense things that others usually can't," Kate wrote. "It seemed that the home's spirits knew Gudrun was coming. Door handles began falling off, lights would burn out and the stove would quit working. Even the toilet wouldn't flush."

And the circus of supernatural activity didn't end once Gudrun arrived—far from it. "During her stay, Gudrun slept downstairs in what had been the home's original parlour," Kate continued. "Late the first night, while the family was asleep, Gudrun was awakened by a man wearing old-fashioned clothing. This manifestation was calling out the name Anne. Gudrun was sure he was walking through the parlour calling, 'Anne, where are you?' "

Completely puzzled by what she had just seen and heard, Gudrun rubbed her eyes. Then she watched, in utter disbelief, as the transparent vision of the man disappeared and another vision appeared before her, this one of a woman lying on a table with flowers all around her. "The scene lasted but a few seconds. Then it was gone," Kate related.

More tired than uneasy, Gudrun finally settled back to sleep. The next day, she mentioned the events to her family. At the first opportunity, they did some checking into the home's previous owners. They came across startling information.

"At the turn of the last century, the wife of a couple living in the house had died at a very young age," Kate wrote. "As was customary in those days, the wake was held in the home. The wife's body was laid out on the table with flowers all around her. But the sad twist to the story is that the husband was out of town at the time of his wife's death and had not been able to get back in time for the funeral."

The man's sorrow over his wife's death, and his grief over his inability to attend her funeral, was so profound that even after his own death he was never fully able to leave their home. But where was Anne buried? The Hanover family asked around, but no one knew.

Years later, when Gudrun was enjoying a leisurely stroll through the nearby Commanda Cemetery, the final piece of the puzzle fell into place. She accidentally came upon the mystery grave. Oddly, she knew it to be Anne's even before she was able to read the name on the marker.

By the time Fran was 15, she had grown weary of living in a haunted house with all of its "bumps in the night." She moved to North Bay, where she boarded with another family. Fran's parents sold the house in the mid-1980s. Up until the very last hours they were in the place, the energies from beyond continued to resonate in that seemingly ordinary home.

Annual Anomaly

Ghosts, by definition, are entities whose energies are able to span the distance of time. Ghosts who have specific time-tables, who seem to relate to the timelines of our own plane of existence, are especially intriguing.

Tom Thomson's apparition (see my *Ontario Ghost Stories*, Lone Pine Publishing, 1998), for example, is most commonly seen on July 8, the anniversary of the day he mysteriously drowned. The descriptions of the sightings are not surprising. Thomson's image is said to be paddling his distinctly coloured canoe near the shoreline of Canoe Lake in Algonquin Park—which is exactly where he died.

A house in Oshawa is home to another excellent example of an annual anomaly. This haunted residence is one of the oldest in the city. Its history—even its ghostly history—has not been well documented, but one story does remain for us to ponder.

On June 27 of each year, beginning at 1:45 AM, phantom knocking noises awaken the living occupant of the house. The strange sounds, which seem to come from the south wall of his bedroom, are always a precursor to a brief but clear appearance by the ghost of a middle-aged man.

The current owner of the house revealed that the spectre seems to "walk out of that south wall." Clad in white, the image from beyond scans the room before walking around it, then disappears once he reaches the point at which he first appeared. Fifty minutes later, the ghost's pattern is repeated in the exact same fashion. This repetition goes on until 5 AM, when the apparition retreats for the last time, not to be seen again until the following year—at the same date and time.

The man who lives in this enigmatic house, and who has done so for more than a quarter of a century now, acknowledges that there are many other ghostly manifestations in his home. The place, he indicates, is well haunted throughout the entire year. Oddly, though, the annual encounter is the only one he was willing to recount for publication.

House Haunter

People frequently ask how I find the stories for my books. The question is simple and seems straightforward, but the answer is fairly complex. I rely upon three methods of information gathering. Sometimes I use just one of them; sometimes I use two or three in combination.

Cold research—that is, simply initiating calls to places that I expect might be haunted—is one way of finding tales. I also write letters to local newspapers requesting that readers send me accounts of their personal experiences with the paranormal. One of my most fruitful sources, though, comes via the grapevine of ghost story lovers.

When ghost story buffs get even the hint of a lead, they often set off immediately on a hunt for the haunting. And they frequently pass on to me the stories they have dug up. The following tale came to be included in this book through the workings of the grapevine. Kate Geisler's co-workers at North Bay's 100.5 EZ ROCK radio station knew that she loves a spooky tale, and they put her in touch with the occupants of a very haunted house in Callander.

Kate visited the house over the Thanksgiving weekend of 2001 and met the people involved in the story. Because her connection with the tale is so close, I present it here almost word for word as she related it to me.

The enthusiastic young radio writer began by explaining a bit about the community in which the paranormal events occurred. "Callander is a small hamlet nestled on the shores of beautiful Lake Nipissing, in Ontario's Blue Sky region," Kate described. "It's a town where families spend lazy summer days on the lake, where ice fishing is the chosen winter pastime and where ghosts have made their home."

She continued, "Talk to the townsfolk and you're sure to hear any number of ghostly tales. One family endured a haunting—months of strange and frightening occurrences—until they could stand it no more. Because Callander is such a small town, I've been asked to change their names."

Linda and Bob (the pseudonyms Kate chose to use) and their three sons lived in an older home on Catherine Street. At the time of the haunting, the boys ranged from pre-school age to high school age. "It all began when one of the younger boys started having friendly conversations with an unseen friend," Kate recalled. "When the lad's parents asked him about his invisible friend, the child responded by telling them only that the person was a man."

After a while, Linda and Bob became concerned about their son's continuing interactions with someone they were unable to see or perceive in any other way. Worse, the entity became bolder, sometimes actually scaring the young child.

As the strength of the spectre's spirit increased, its ghostly hijinks became noticeable to the rest of the household. Linda and Bob would smell perfume in their home when there was no reason for such an aroma. They would pass through cold spots and hear the echo of disembodied footsteps along the floors.

Inside doors would open and close without any help. Lights would mysteriously flicker. And Linda even noticed a kitchen chair creak as an unseen someone sat down on it. All the while, the younger son kept on talking to his friend, the phantom—especially at night.

The enigmatic events created an unpleasant change in the atmosphere of this small-town Ontario household. Sharing their lives with unexplained forces began to take its toll on the couple. Kate acknowledged that "Linda and Bob's marriage was definitely feeling the strain of their unwanted house guest. The couple quarreled more, and Linda, much to her own horror, began having thoughts about leaving her husband."

Then one day, while in the living room, Linda noticed that a crucifix that normally lay on the shelf of an entertainment unit was standing upright. Her younger boys were too little to reach the cross, so the situation puzzled her. Not knowing what else she could or should do, she simply reached up, repositioned the item and left the room.

Moments later, Linda came back into the living room and was startled to see "that the crucifix was once again standing upright on the shelf. Feeling understandably unnerved, she lay the ornament down once more and again left the room." By this time Linda was concerned enough that she discussed the incidents with her husband, a man who, up to that point, was a committed skeptic. Much to her surprise, Bob admitted that he, too, "had noticed the crucifix standing upright on the shelf."

Linda and Bob now realized that something was very wrong in their home. They just didn't know what that something was. Hoping to gather information, they asked their oldest son if he'd ever experienced anything out of the ordinary. The young man's answer did nothing to assuage their fears, for he, too, had been having close encounters with the presence.

"One evening," Kate revealed, "the teenager had watched in amazement as the fridge door slowly opened, then closed, of its own accord." And once, "while on the front porch of his home waiting for his girlfriend…he felt a presence near him. Thinking it was his girlfriend sneaking up on him, he turned and found himself face-to-face with an old gentleman—a transparent old gentleman."

Unless the younger boy had seen the image to which he so regularly talked, this was the first sighting of the entity. The older lad stood, temporarily paralyzed with fear, until the ghost disappeared. Then, not surprisingly, the teenager also disappeared as quickly as he was able to—by running into the house.

Because it takes a great deal of strength for a ghost to become visible, the resident phantom was obviously gaining power. And the family was about to be given proof of that fact. In an attempt to objectively document the increasingly strange situation, Linda and Bob devised a plan. "One day, on the advice of Linda's brother, they set up a cassette recorder," Kate explained. "They then took their sons and left their house. A few hours passed before the family returned."

When they got back to the house, the adults played the cassette tape to discover if there had been any phantom sounds in the home during their absence. "What they heard when they replayed the tape sent shivers up and down Linda's spine," Kate recalled. "There were sounds of doors opening and closing, of footsteps, and then, the scariest of all, a whispering voice that appeared to be saying, 'Get out.' For Linda, this was the last straw."

Badly shaken, the woman felt she had no choice but to contact a man named Manuel whom a friend had recommended. This potential helper could, according to what Linda's friend had heard, "rid their home of spirits."

Kate explained that "Manuel has more than 50 years of experience as a psychic healer. He also sees spirits and can remove them. During Manuel's first visit to the home, he sensed some very bad presences." So bad, in fact, that the visit left even the experienced exorcist shaken.

"Manuel, Bob, Linda and their children were outside talking when Manuel saw the figure of a boy standing next to a neighbouring garage." The boy's image talked to Manuel, pleading for the older man's help.

The psychic asked Linda and Bob if either of them could see or hear the apparition that was talking to him. Both husband and wife tried, but neither could see or hear what Manuel could. The manifestation vaporized shortly after its appearance and, although it wasn't the phantom they had set out to look for, there was now no question that at least one needy spirit resided near the family's home.

During her visit with the couple on that long autumn weekend in 2001, Linda and Bob explained to Kate that "one of Manuel's first jobs was to cleanse the family members themselves of any bad spirits. Having done that, the psychically gifted man moved inside the house, with Bob right behind him all the way reading from the Bible. Manuel burned incense as he made his way through the rooms. At one point in time, the spirits pushed Manuel to his knees. All the while Bob stayed at his assignment, keeping himself behind the man and reading from the Bible."

What happened next was something that no one involved with the attempted exorcism would ever forget. "Manuel reported seeing the spirit of the boy from next door in Linda and Bob's home. He was requesting Manuel's help to cross over from this world to the place he belonged. He had been trapped for many years and didn't know how to make the journey. The boy's spirit was frustrated and angry."

Manuel determined that it was the negative energy of this ghost's anger that had caused other unwanted spirits to haunt Linda and Bob's home. When the expunging process was finished and the final count tallied, the family realized that Manuel had cleansed their home of five different ghosts.

Manuel made an assertion that I have never heard before but which I certainly cannot dismiss given the man's experience and credentials. Souls, he told the couple, "always travel in odd numbers, never even." An intriguing piece of supernatural information, to be sure.

Kate concluded her telling of the events that had so shaken this family's lives by explaining that after Manuel had cleansed their home, Linda, Bob and their children all noticed an immediate improvement in the atmosphere of the place. The house "didn't seem heavy and oppressed" as it had previously been, but "felt warm and comfortable, like a home should."

To this day "Linda truly feels that Manuel is a lifesaver." By cleansing their home of the spirits and sending those lost souls to the great beyond where they could find their eternal rest, he rescued the five family members from a possible future of untold supernatural agony.

A Haunted House in Hamilton

From the outside, the Roddicks' home on Martha Street in Hamilton's East End looked much the same as other houses on the street. From the inside, it was set apart by a resident ghost.

The Roddicks and this spirit co-existed in the dwelling from 1966 until 1985. Perhaps they wouldn't have lived there together quite so long if the haunting had been a constant phenomenon but, as Kim Roddick explained, "the ghost chose not to make itself known all the time, just once in a while."

"When the ghost did choose to make itself known," Kim continued, "it made sure we knew it was there." And then the young woman proceeded to describe some of the spectre's antics.

Kim's brother, David, experienced what was probably the most bizarre encounter with the phantom. He heard the sounds of a person whistling as he or she walked up the stairs. He never saw the presence, but was able to follow the invisible being's path as "whatever it was entered his room and then exited—through the closed window."

David and his other sister, Heather, had a joint encounter when they were both quite young. "They were standing outside the bathroom when the water in the tub turned on. Not just a dribble, but full force, as if someone was drawing a bath. They argued about who would go in to turn it off, and agreed that Heather, who was a year older, would lead and David would follow. They went in, and Heather's hand was just inches from the tap when the water stopped flowing just as quickly as it had begun. Both said they didn't see the faucet turn; they just saw the water stopping."

David was involved in another paranormal experience when he was a teenager. "When he was about 15, David had just crawled into bed one night. He heard some high-pitched whistling downstairs. It wasn't a tune or anything, just a monotone whistle. At first he thought it was the pipes, because they tended to do that. But then the sound moved up the stairs. Before it arrived at the top of the stairs near his bedroom door, David shut his eyes tight.

"The sound moved into David's room, then stopped moving just inside the door. David said that although he was too afraid to open his eyes, he had the sensation that something was staring at him, almost as though it was surprised to see him. Eventually it moved across the room to the window and faded away."

That spooky experience had a permanent effect on Kim's brother: more than 20 years later, David still closes his door before going to bed. But other occurrences became quite commonplace within the home. Over the years, members of the household grew accustomed to some of the noises the ghost made.

"On a regular basis we would hear footsteps upstairs when there was no one up there," Kim described. "At first we passed it off as the floorboards settling, but the rhythm of the sounds and the fact that they moved across the floor made that explanation unlikely."

When Kim's sisters were teenagers, they were awakened one night by the ghostly footsteps. "Heather and Cheryl heard a loud banging coming up the stairs. Both were too frightened to get out of bed. Finally Cheryl, who is two years older than Heather, jumped out of bed just before the banging got to the top of the stairs. She closed the door and jumped back into bed. Then the banging stopped. There was no one there."

Kim's parents were also aware of the ghost's presence. "One day my father was talking. He said something spooky, as he often did. As if on cue, the front door swung open and the back door slammed shut almost simultaneously. To this day, none of us who were there can remember exactly what it was my father said that seemed to have sparked the commotion."

More than just the people in the family were affected by the haunting. As is often the case, the family pet—in this case, a dog—was keenly aware of the spirit whenever it was around. "He would be nervous about going down to the basement," Kim recalled. "He would bark at something down there."

Despite several thorough examinations of the area, the Roddicks were never able to determine what it was the dog was sensing. "The basement door would swing closed when it had been open, and swing open when it had been closed, even when it had been secured tightly. Of course, we tried to pass this mystery off as having been caused by drafts from the basement—but drafts don't turn doorknobs."

When the family moved, the ghost with whom they'd shared the house for nearly 20 years did not follow them. Its presence was clearly attached to that otherwise ordinary house; sometime later, Mrs. Roddick, Kim's mother, had the opportunity to speak with the new residents of the house. They told her that they, too, had weathered some unexplained occurrences in the house. In fact, they were convinced the place was haunted!

The memories of growing up in the haunted house followed the Roddicks, giving all of them ready-made stories to tell their future grandchildren.

The Night Knocker

Laura and Dennis, together with their small son, Bradley, were delighted when they purchased their home in the Timmins area. The place was beautiful, and Ann, Laura's sister, could live there, too, which made the situation nearly perfect. Ann's friend, a woman I shall refer to only as K, was my correspondent for this story. K has firsthand knowledge of many of the episodes I am about to describe because she spent an eventful night in the haunted house.

K assured me that the home, built atop a small hill overlooking a lake, is attractive and unique. Its interior is steeped in character and equally as appealing as its lovely setting. Decorative mouldings grace the walls and doorways. The original hardwood flooring has been maintained. And a multitude of windows let sun stream in from almost every angle, giving the house a cheery quality.

The exquisite features of the building are topped by a lovely grand staircase leading to and from the upstairs. The whole place is so charming, K said, that when she first saw it, she thought "it almost seemed impossible that anything out of the ordinary could happen in a house such as this."

The most intriguing aspect of Dennis and Laura's home, for ghost lovers anyway, is the presence of an invisible resident—or possibly residents. The first rather unusual thing the couple noticed was that their little boy, Bradley, was spending a considerable amount of time "talking to imaginary friends." When questioned about his partners in conversation, he declared that there were two of them—an old man and a little girl.

Neither Bradley's discussions nor his explanations about the "people" with whom he was having them really upset

Laura and Dennis. But the conversations did serve as a subtle warning about what was soon to become commonplace in their house.

One day, Laura was in the basement doing chores. Preoccupied with the tasks at hand, it took her a few seconds to realize that she'd seen an unexpected movement in the periphery of her vision. Turning to face the area where the activity had originated, the woman was astonished to see that the lid on her box of laundry detergent was flapping madly about without anyone around it.

Rather than denying the likelihood that she was living in a haunted house, Laura simply did the polite thing—she gave the resident spirit a name: Cecil. Whether the ghost was the appropriate gender for the name, and whether the spirit was the only supernatural being at work in the building, he or she seemed to appreciate being acknowledged. The spectre even expressed its gratitude shortly thereafter.

On an otherwise unremarkable day, Laura was alone in the home doing laundry. She put a load of dirty clothes into the washing machine, turned it on and made a mental note to herself to transfer the wet, washed clothes into the dryer in less than an hour. But Laura was busy with other chores and more than an hour passed before she gave the laundry another thought. When she did go downstairs to pull the wet clothes out of the washer and put them in the dryer, she found to her amazement that the transfer had already been done. Because Laura knew for a fact that no one else had been in the house, she presumed the ghost was just giving her a helping hand.

Other phantom activities that occurred could be described as being, at best, more playful. Sometimes, in fact, they could be downright annoying. Laura and Dennis explained to K that "hats have moved from peg to peg on the wall rack. The shower curtain has on several occasions been torn from its bar and left lying on the floor. The oven [seems] hot even when it is not turned on and has not been used for some time."

To tolerate the disruptions that living with a ghost can bring, most people need to have a calm and accepting way about them. After all, little in our lives is more personal than the sanctity of our home. The same can be said for our names. A ghost in the beautiful home on the hill managed to invade that highly personal boundary also. On another day when Laura knew for certain that she was alone in the house, she clearly heard a disembodied voice calling her name.

"Laura descended to the basement and suddenly things changed," K described. "A tightness gripped her chest unlike anything she'd ever felt before. It was as if the breath was literally being sucked out of her, or that she was caught in a vice grip. The feeling was so overwhelming that she retreated once again to the main floor." What happened then was equally amazing: when she returned to the kitchen, the feeling she had just experienced suddenly subsided.

Knowing of K's fascination with the paranormal, Laura and Dennis invited the woman to spend the night in their haunted house. The first hint for K that this visit was going to be a supernatural adventure came shortly after she entered the home. She described that initial clue as "generally, a feeling that we were not alone in the house. I felt that someone was constantly watching us."

After escorting K on a tour of the building, the family continued on with their normal activities. At one point, Ann was upstairs bathing little Bradley. Suddenly, everyone else in the household was shocked to hear her panicked yells. Laura, Dennis and K all stopped what they had been doing and ran as fast as they could to Ann's side at the tub. They found the woman visibly shaken. She said she had heard someone call out her name.

Once everyone's heart rates had returned to normal, the four adults carried on with their evening. When it was finally bedtime, K "had the honour of retiring to the 'haunted' or 'creepy' room on the main floor while everyone else headed upstairs." Although not frightened by anything specific, K immediately realized that she felt considerably less comfortable alone than she had when the others had been nearby. The expression "safety in numbers" took on a whole new meaning.

Despite the notable absence of flesh-and-blood companionship, K did what she could to make herself comfortable. "I snuggled up under the cozy duvet, noticing the bright brass headboard above me," she described. "My mind was still reeling with all that I had heard and felt that day when suddenly a 'tap, tap, tap' came from the wall above my head. It was the headboard tapping lightly against the wall. Not moving a muscle, I continued to listen. The sound started up again. 'Tap, tap, tap.' "

K had made a point of lying completely still, so she knew for a fact that the tapping sounds had nothing to do with any movement she might have made. "Summoning the courage to investigate on my own," she continued, "I decided to try to make the headboard tap by myself. Wriggling, jiggling and crazy rocking could not make that headboard tap against the wall."

K may have been horrified by the situation she found herself in, but that fear did nothing to dampen her sense of humour. "The sight of me on all fours trying to make that bed move must have given Cecil a chuckle," she declared. Possibly so, but it didn't produce the desired effect. None of K's actions could replicate the tapping sounds she had heard.

At that point, the woman's practical side came to the fore. "The night was late and I was tired; in all honesty, I only wanted sleep," she confessed. "I grabbed a quilted throw from beside the bed and stuffed it between the headboard and the wall." This action managed to stop, or at least muffle, the sounds that had been frightening K. She was finally able to drift off to the land of Nod, but she admitted that at best she slept fitfully that night.

The next morning, K decided immediately that she was going to head home to her own, unhaunted house.

Laura and her family still reside in the Timmins area home. Every so often, something inexplicable still happens. For the most part, though, the family has become very used to the advantages and disadvantages of living in a house haunted by a ghost they affectionately call Cecil.

Living with Miss Glover

This story came to me in one of my favourite ways. A man who received a copy of my book *Ontario Ghost Stories* (Lone Pine Publishing, 1998) as a gift wrote to give me an update on one of the tales included in it. In the same letter, he also told me of his own encounters with the paranormal.

Robert "Bob" Mowers, who now lives in Sutton on the south shore of Lake Simcoe, informed me that in October of 2000 he had been "in the house on the northeast corner of Yonge Street and the Stouffville Sideroad—an ice cream place called Legge's." Bob had once read that the place was haunted and he was unable to resist inquiring about its current status.

"I asked the guy serving me if Homer [the ghost] was still around, and he said that the spirit was absolutely still in the house," he recalled. "The guy who served me seemed very interested that I knew about Homer—even that I knew his body was not buried with his family members."

Since that visit, the building has changed hands once again. According to Bob, it is now "an equestrian riding place that sells saddles, etc." There's no word on whether or not the haunting remains active.

After opening with that interesting follow-up to a previous story, Bob Mowers proceeded to detail some of the encounters he and his family experienced from 1982 to 1987 while they were living in a very haunted house in Aurora. "This was a period of my life I will truly never forget," he declared. "I don't often talk about it because people think I'm nuts or something, so I would usually just avoid it. However, if someone asks me about it, I will discuss it with passion."

When Bob and his then-wife, Donna, bought the house in the town on Highway 11, approximately halfway between Newmarket and Richmond Hill, they had no inkling that the place came with a resident spirit. "Nothing was said to us about the ghost," Bob wrote. "I did find it very odd, however, that three families had moved out within a year and a half prior to our buying it."

Such a high turnover rate was odd because the property was unusually attractive. "The house is located on Catherine Avenue, one of the oldest streets in Aurora," Bob described. "It is a very beautiful street with mature maple trees that overhang on both sides of the roadway. The house is a two-and-a-half-storey red brick home built by James Albert Knowles, a mason and builder by trade. Mr. Knowles built other homes on Catherine Avenue, but this one was made for his own family. The house remained in the Knowles family for 47 years, from 1913 to 1959. Four different Knowles families lived there."

After that long run of stability, some changes were inevitable, but what was to develop went far beyond the expected. "Subsequently, ownership changed hands eight times, most noticeably from 1979 to 1982, when five families moved in and out in quick succession," Bob explained.

Even with that information, neither Bob nor Donna jumped to the conclusion that the place might be haunted. Instead they felt that there must be a structural problem. To guard against making an expensive mistake, they arranged to have the house inspected before they submitted an offer to purchase. The building inspector advised that the house was structurally sound and that the roof and wiring had been upgraded.

This report was good news. Bob and Donna's concerns seemed to have been unwarranted. Relieved and pleased, they bought the place and moved into it very shortly thereafter. Although he didn't know it at the time, Bob's first encounter with a previous occupant of the home came just two days later.

Bob explained, "I was upstairs moving boxes around in the finished attic when I felt a presence near my left shoulder. I was shocked and felt goosebumps. The hair on the back of my neck stood up. It felt like there was someone standing right behind me. I even felt the breathing!" Hoping to find an acceptable explanation for his uncomfortable feelings, Bob called to Donna and asked if she'd been upstairs. She yelled back from the kitchen and said that she had not been up in the attic.

Little did Bob suspect that this odd experience was only the first of many. "That same thing occurred at various times during the first couple of weeks and always while moving boxes around and starting to sort things out in the attic," Bob wrote. Then he described another strange incident.

"A few days after moving in, I cut the lawn for the first time. At the left rear of the backyard, I discovered a very precise depression in the ground about two inches deep. It was rectangular in shape, like a shoebox, and caught my attention because the lawn mower got stuck in it. Given the look of the thing, it appeared that something may have been buried there."

Bob's curiosity got the best of him. "I proceeded to dig that piece of ground up, but I went down about a foot and found nothing," he continued. "I figured that if something had been buried there, it had long since decayed." Ever practical, Bob filled in the hole he had dug and "planted a tree there so the lawn mower would no longer get stuck in the depression."

Revealing a decidedly analytical bent, Bob noted that after this episode "a pattern began to emerge" in the house. "There was a cycle to the ghostly occurrences. Things always began to happen in the fall. September, October and November occurrences were on a daily, or every other day, basis. During the winter, spring and summer months almost nothing happened."

The ghost seemed to provide only an occasional reminder of its ongoing presence. Bob assessed that the spirit "just wanted to let us know it was still around." Understandably curious, the man decided to investigate the history of the house, to find out if perhaps a death had occurred there during some long-ago autumn. He approached the staff at the Aurora Historical Society, but the information they dug up did not include anything about a death in the house during any season of any year.

The researchers did discover that a spinster named Miss Glover had purchased the house in 1965. The woman and her family of cats lived there until the woman's death in 1971. Bob had unknowingly found the first evidence of Miss Glover's association with his home when he discovered the backyard depression.

At the time, though, Bob and Donna were not looking for any signs. They were still holding on to the hope that there was a logical explanation for the decidedly strange events they were experiencing. They continued to put these occurrences down to coincidence. This rationalization worked for them for a while, but soon, due to the sheer volume of incidents, there was just no possible way to keep writing them off as mere oddities.

One such incident occurred during the first autumn season the Mowerses lived in the house. Bob recalled that the home had a fireplace in it that they very much enjoyed using. "On a typical Friday evening I lit a nice fire and we sat near it and talked," he wrote. What followed one of those quiet weekend rituals was anything but typical.

On this particular night, Donna went upstairs to bed at about 11 PM and Bob stayed up a little later. He sat around for a while, then closed the chimney flue and the fireplace screen. In doing so, he noted that the ashes from that evening's fire and many previous fires lay on the floor of the hearth.

The next morning, Bob was awake and downstairs before his wife. As he walked past the fireplace, he was startled to see that although the flue and the screen were still closed, all the ashes had been put into a neat pile in front of the fireplace on the family room floor. There were no ashes left in the hearth at all.

Completely baffled by what he was seeing, Bob called up to his wife to see if she had been downstairs yet, but she said no. Demonstrating his mastery of the understatement, Bob concluded his description of the event with the phrase, "It was most unusual."

Donna, too, had encounters with the spirit—not all of them comfortable. When Bob was at work and she was alone in the house, the woman would periodically hear her guitar being played, always when she was on one floor and the guitar was on another. This phenomenon was unnerving enough to Donna that she would occasionally phone Bob at work and ask him to come home.

A phantom light band mysteriously appeared in this photo taken inside a haunted house.

One unsettling phantom prank took place in the late fall. This time Donna didn't even think of phoning Bob. She was absolutely positive that the sounds of the front door opening and closing, followed by footsteps climbing the staircase to the second floor, were merely an indication of her husband's arrival home from work. Even the timing was right—it was 5:05 PM, the time Bob routinely arrived home. Donna called out a welcoming greeting. When she received no response, she became worried that an intruder was upstairs in the house.

Some 25 minutes later, Bob walked in the front door of his home to find his wife "looking as white as a ghost." She quickly explained that she'd heard someone come into the house and go upstairs. Because she'd heard nothing since then, she presumed the trespasser was still on the second floor. Bob confessed, "I was freaking out! I was scared."

Donna's husband loaded his shotgun and climbed the stairs. "My heart was beating like crazy," he wrote. "I went into every room and looked in every possible nook and cranny—anywhere a person might be able to hide. I found nothing."

Convinced that there was no stranger in the house, Bob joined Donna downstairs. Sadly for her peace of mind, she remained sure of what she'd heard and maintained that someone other than the two of them must be in the house. When the remainder of the evening and night passed by with no inexplicable disturbances, however, the incident was eventually shoved to the back of her mind.

Of course, even for people living with something puzzling, life must go on. So it was for Bob and Donna. They became the proud and happy parents of a daughter named Elly. And two years later, they were blessed with a son, Graham.

Children are usually more aware of the presence of paranormal beings than adults are, but such was not the case in this instance. Neither Elly nor Graham seemed to be affected by the ghost that was bothering their parents. Some years after they moved from the house, Graham told his father that "a young boy would often come and visit him in his bedroom at bedtime."

Before Graham was even born, Bob witnessed the only really terrifying encounter with a resident wraith. Donna was out that particular evening and Bob was putting baby Elly to bed. The nightly routine began in a peaceful way. Bob fed the little girl, took her into her bedroom, changed her clothes and then sat with her in the rocking chair across the room from her crib.

"It was very quiet," Bob wrote, "just the two of us rocking in the rocking chair. I sang to her. The window and drapes were closed." Happily relaxed, holding his sleeping infant, Bob was totally unprepared for what happened next. "Suddenly, the crib lifted up to a height where the bottom of its legs were at least a foot off the floor and it banged against the wall."

The movements were intense and forceful; whatever was causing them was very powerful. The bizarre activity went on "strongly and loudly for some 30 seconds," Bob wrote. "Then the crib suddenly just fell to the floor and became perfectly still." Bob candidly admitted that this event "scared the hell out of me."

Bob's initial reaction after witnessing this supernatural demonstration was one of denial. But seconds later, still cradling Elly, he got up and fled. "I couldn't put her to bed in that crib, so I took her downstairs and put on the TV. I watched TV until 2 AM, at which time I finally took Elly back to her room. I sat in the rocking chair with her for half an hour to see if the crib would start jumping again."

All seemed normal in the room, so Bob lay the little girl in her bed. Still not entirely assured that his daughter would be safe, he sat back down in the rocking chair by himself for another 30 minutes. When all remained calm, he finally went to bed himself. "This only happened once and never again," he concluded, "but what an impact it had. What a memory!"

After Graham was born, Bob was witness to a different type of bedtime occurrence. "I recall many times rocking my son to sleep in his bedroom, the only one in the house with a dimmer light switch in it," he wrote. As the two rocked peacefully back and forth in the chair, the brightness of the lightbulb dimmed, eventually fading to darkness—although no one had been near the switch.

Doobie, the family dog, might have been left with some strange memories, too. At times, when no one else in the household could either see or sense anything unusual, Doobie would bark like crazy while staring at a particular spot. He was clearly disturbed by something or someone not detectable to the human members of the family.

Three distinctly different encounters took place in bathrooms in the haunted house. In the upstairs bathroom, Bob would often hear a human being sigh. The sound came from some invisible source that was very close to him at the time—either beside or behind him. Bob added, "That sound was always there. I could not make out if it was male or female."

Just as regularly, while washing his hands at the sink in the bathroom under the staircase, Bob would see a reflection in the mirror, an image of someone walking very quickly through the hall past the washroom. Despite his efforts to find the source of the image, no readily understandable explanation was ever found.

During an evening when Bob and Donna were entertaining two other couples, one of the men excused himself and went to that same main-floor bathroom. A simple enough procedure, it would seem, but getting himself back out of the washroom proved to be extremely difficult. "He was unable to open the door," Bob explained. "He said it felt just like there was someone on the other side of the door pressing up against it and holding it closed."

Thinking that his friends were playing a joke on him, the man became angry. He yelled through the door, informing his friends that he did not share their sense of humour and demanding to be let free. But Donna, Bob, the other visiting couple and the trapped man's wife were all sitting in the family room. No one had been anywhere near that bathroom door.

Whatever force had been holding the guest captive in the bathroom suddenly vanished, and the door flew open. The man stayed with the others at the Mowerses home for the balance of the evening, probably still under the impression that he had been the brunt of a practical joke. He may have been annoyed, but he clearly didn't hold a grudge because sometime later he and his wife were back visiting Bob and Donna for an evening of cards in the dining room.

"Suddenly [the same man] stood up and ran out of the house," Bob wrote. "He left his wife here." Bob kindly drove the woman home and the next day the male guest explained his odd action. "He said he was suddenly overcome by a very strange feeling in the house," Bob wrote. "He did not know exactly what it was, but he said that he felt he had to get out in a hurry."

That experience was undeniably mystifying, but compounding the puzzle were two other factors. First, Bob and Donna had made a point of not telling friends that they had suspicions about their house being haunted. Second, no one else sitting at the table had detected anything out of the ordinary. The bizarre event involving the male guest remained one of the many never-to-be-solved mysteries involving the house on Catherine Avenue.

Donna's Aunt Shirley was also a guest in the haunted home. Perhaps because she was a relative, Bob and Donna were more forthcoming with her about their ghost than they had been with their friends. Shirley was not psychic, but she was kind, sensitive and open-minded. The woman asked the couple if they'd ever experimented with automatic writing— that is, simply sitting at a desk with a pen poised over a pad of paper, ready to write whatever message came to mind. During the heyday of spiritualism in this country, automatic writing was a very popular way of receiving messages from those on another plane.

Bob and Donna were admittedly intrigued. Donna was the first to try it. After about 10 minutes, her hand began moving on the page. Then, after a few minutes of movement, it stopped. Donna's aunt and husband were both curious to see if anything intelligible had come through, but according to Bob, "it appeared to be just a lot of scribbling."

Bob's turn was next. "We all saw my arm and hand moving," he wrote. "After a while, I looked at the paper and again there was just a bunch of scribbles." Not to be left out, Aunt Shirley decided to try. She picked up the pen and held it to the paper. Immediately the older woman's arm began to move. When it stopped moving there were no mindless scribbles on the page. Far from it. There, on the paper, as clear as could be, was a single word: DEVIL. That revelation put a hasty stop to the whole experiment.

A photograph of a ghost is an extremely rare article, but in Bob and Donna's family album there are several snapshots with odd markings on them—the kind of markings that are usually associated with the disturbances in energy that a ghost creates when it is present. "The oddest one was taken on Christmas morning," Bob explained. "Elly was opening her present beside the Christmas tree. In the

The spirit in this house apparently wanted to be part of the Christmas fun.

photograph she is sitting on the floor and there is a strong, bright energy source beside her. It's about a foot off the ground. It's some sort of a beam of light in an odd sort of circular shape."

Hoping to find a sensible answer for such a strange mark, Bob had the camera checked out. It was found to be in proper working order. The technician attested that there was nothing in the workings of the camera that would have created such an effect.

Thinking that perhaps a psychic might be able to explain the image in the snapshot, Bob took a trip to the Scarborough Psychic Centre. "I spoke with a gentleman named John," he wrote. "He amazed me with his accuracy. At one point during our hour-long conversation, I asked him if he could tell me anything about my house. He paused for about 15 seconds, during which time he appeared to be deep in thought."

When the psychic spoke again, his words took Bob by surprise. "It's a much older house. It's red brick," John began. Bob confirmed that both statements were correct. The psychic's next comment seemed strange to Bob: "Does your wife own a sewing machine?" Donna did not own one and Bob was curious as to why John would make such an inquiry. The man's explanation only served to confound Bob even more. He said, "Because I see an older lady treadling on an old-fashioned sewing machine in this house."

Confusing as it may have been, Bob's investigation was beginning to give some insight into the spirit who was haunting his house. And that was a good thing, because it wasn't too long before Bob was allowed a glimpse of the ghost.

Early one evening, Bob was engaged in a telephone conversation. While he talked, he glanced out a window and saw what he describes as "a bizarre-looking woman coming up the driveway, heading toward the back door. She was dressed in a long, flowing robe. She was all in white, except for the wide-brimmed hat she was wearing. The hat was about 1.5 metres wide and had many multicoloured things sticking out of it."

Bob was shocked, but presumed that the woman outside was "associated with a strange religious denomination." Because he was on the phone, he was not immediately available to deal with the visitor, so he called to Donna, who was upstairs at the time. He asked her to come down, advised her that a very strange-looking woman was coming to the back door and cautioned her to be careful as the person appeared to be a religious fanatic of some sort.

Oddly, no knock on the door followed the woman-in-white's walk toward the house. And when Donna came downstairs and opened the back door, no one was waiting there. Thinking that the stranger could not have gone far in those few seconds, Bob's wife walked out into the backyard and looked in the garage. No one was on or even near the property.

While this incident was indeed enigmatic, Bob was most surprised by his reaction. "I felt uneasy about this, and after quite some time realized that what bothered me was that the image did not walk up the driveway but just seemed to float by the window. I only saw her for a few seconds, but I do remember that the dress or robe she was wearing was flowing or blowing in the wind."

Bob decided that this was an isolated incident and did his best to put it out of his mind. To a very large degree, he succeeded—right up until August 1991, when he was advised by a co-worker that during a visit to the house many years earlier, the co-worker's wife and another friend had seen a similar apparition—a woman in a white wedding dress walking up the driveway toward the back door.

No explanation, supernatural or otherwise, was ever found for the bizarre visitations. But another woman who visited—one who was very much alive—was helpful in answering some of the growing number of questions the Mowers family had about their old home. The woman's name was Emily, and she had lived in the house on Catherine Avenue from 1973 to 1979. Bob took her on a tour of the place so she could see what they'd done to her former home.

"To this point neither of us had mentioned anything about a ghost," Bob wrote. "As she was about to leave I said to her, 'Emily, before you leave, there is one question I would like to ask you about the house.' She said to me, 'I already know what you're going to ask. You're going to ask if it's haunted.' "

Bob admitted that was exactly the question he had in mind. Emily's reply was swift and sure. She told the man that the house was "very definitely haunted" and that she and the other members of her family had encountered many inexplicable events during their seven years living there.

Bob recounted for Emily all the incidents he and Donna had experienced since moving into the house. He included in his story a mention of Miss Glover, the woman who had owned the home before Emily did. It turned out that Emily knew about Miss Glover and was able to supplement Bob's knowledge about the former proprietor.

"Her cats were her whole life; she was totally dedicated to them," Emily explained. Then she added that when one of Miss Glover's pets died, the woman would bury the animal's body on the property. She had even left written instructions that those little graves were never to be disturbed. Unfortunately, that note had disappeared by the time Bob and Donna had purchased the property and Bob had, no doubt, unwittingly disturbed one of those final resting spots when he dug up the precisely defined depression in the lawn and planted a tree there.

Some pieces of this puzzle were beginning to come together. Bob and Donna were still a very long way from arriving at any definitive answers, but at least they now had confirmation that they weren't the only people to have been disturbed by the presence in their house.

Being social people, the Mowerses enjoyed entertaining and, toward that end, they decided to host a Halloween party. Their next-door neighbours supplied a rather interesting item of decoration—a coffin. Bringing such an artifact into an already haunted house might have been an invitation for trouble, but the party went well.

At the end of the festivities, Donna decided to go around the house and take down the Halloween decorations they had put up. Unfortunately, she wasn't able to do so. None of the witch figures, caricatures of ghosts or images of jack-o'-lanterns would budge when she tried to peel them off the walls. The woman quite sensibly decided to postpone the chore until the following morning—except that by then it was too late. The next morning every one of the decorations was found on the floor.

The last ghostly event Bob witnessed in the house involved an extremely strong psychic projection that occurred just before the Mowers family moved away from Catherine Avenue. Bob emphasized that the move was not in any way associated with the presence of the ghost, but he admitted that this episode troubled him deeply.

"I really thought I was losing my mind this time!" Bob wrote. "One evening, Donna was out…I was washing dishes when I suddenly heard a loud voice coming from the basement. It yelled my name—'BOB!!!' It really startled me. I stopped what I was doing and went downstairs, but found nothing out of the ordinary."

Because there was little else the man could do by way of investigating the source of the sound, Bob merely returned to the kitchen to finish his chore. But the adventure was far from over.

"A few minutes later, I heard something so weird that I thought I had lost it for sure," Bob continued. "I heard, from the basement below me, a tea party going on! Again, I stopped what I was doing and listened. I heard three elderly sounding female voices. They were talking loudly and laughing, seemingly having a really good time. Every sound was very clear. I could hear three different voices. I also heard when a cup was put on a saucer and when they were stirring the tea in their cups. Every sound was there—very loud."

Despite Bob's concentrated effort to make out what the three phantom voices were discussing, he was unsuccessful: "No words were clear. They were all gibberish." Demonstrating a goodly amount of courage, he made a second trip down to the basement, but he'd apparently missed the party. All was quiet, with nothing out of the ordinary to be seen or heard.

Not long after this extremely strange event, the Mowers family moved out of the house on Catherine Avenue. Through local scuttlebutt, Donna heard that Mr. and Mrs. B, the people who bought the old house, had it exorcised. Bob's curiosity was piqued when he learned of this ceremony, so he paid a call to his former home. The new owner readily confirmed that a cleansing ritual had been performed by a church leader in the company of his wife.

During the exorcism ceremony, the minister advised the spirit that it no longer belonged on this plane and it should move "on toward the light." The man spoke and prayed in each room of the house. When the procedure was over, the homeowners, the preacher and the preacher's wife were gathered in the front hall when they all heard a female voice scream loudly.

For a second, the four stood in stunned silence. Then the minister spoke, advising the homeowners that the ear-piercing wail they'd all just heard had been the ghost. "She's gone," he stated simply, and then predicted that any problems associated with the haunting were now a thing of the past.

The minister had done his job effectively; his words were prophetic. From that time to the present date, nothing at all out of the ordinary has happened.

Today, Bob Mowers lives a little farther north in Sutton. His current house is even older than the one on Catherine Avenue, but it is not haunted. Bob acknowledges that after the excitement of living with a ghost, he misses having the added dimension in his life.

Bob's paranormal encounters are some of the most intriguing I've ever heard.

Madeline the House Haunter

Kelly agreed to have her first name used in the telling of her experiences while living in a haunted house, but she insisted that her last name be excluded from the story. To protect their anonymity, Kelly also requested that her husband, her husband's sister, the sister's son and the sister's boyfriend not be named. For clarity, I have arbitrarily chosen to refer to Kelly's husband as Dan and Dan's sister as Joan. Joan's three-year-old son shall be known as Brody and Joan's boyfriend shall be called Sam.

The strange events began in the mid-1990s when Kelly and Dan moved into a quaint little home on Copeland Street in North Bay. At first the couple had no idea that their new accommodations would bring them more than basic shelter. How could they know that the home would also provide them with hours of puzzling entertainment?

As is often the case, the household pet was the first to become aware that something quite out of the ordinary was taking place in the dwelling. Kelly explained that one day, "while [Dan and I were] chatting with friends in the living room of the house, the dog began acting in a peculiar fashion. Its hackles stood up on end and the animal began growling and barking and staring into the dining room."

My informant and her husband, along with their guests, were disturbed enough by this spontaneous ruckus that they stopped their conversation, looked at the dog and then followed the pet's gaze into the dining room—where a bamboo chair that had been suspended from the ceiling in the dining room was swinging madly about.

The little group sat and stared in stunned silence for a moment. What could be causing this bizarre occurrence? "No windows were open, there was no breeze and no one was visible in the room. Despite the seeming impossibility of movement under those circumstances, the chair continued to swing back and forth of its own volition at breakneck speed. And then, without warning, it suddenly stopped moving, dead in mid-swing, and hung perfectly still."

Oddly, the poor dog was even more affected when the chair stopped moving than it was when the movement started. The little animal began to cower and whimper, then ran away with its tail tucked in between its legs.

After animals, the beings most sensitive to the presence of a ghost are children. When Joan, Sam and Brody moved in with Kelly and Dan, everyone became much more aware of the resident revenant. Brody began to ask some very strange questions—questions the likes of which the boy had never asked before. One day he demanded to know who the man at the door was and why he just flew out the window! My correspondent acknowledged that "this comment left the others wide-eyed and stunned."

Despite their growing concern about what forces might be at work in their new home, none of the adult residents of the house was able to think of any way to get help or advice. So they kept the information about the situation to themselves until, by coincidence, Kelly was out and about in town one day and happened to meet the past owners of the home.

Kelly was in for the surprise of her life when one of the previous occupants of the house asked if she had "met Madeline yet." Even though Kelly was shocked, she was also somewhat relieved. She now had a name for the spirit with whom she shared a home. And she had confirmation that all of the bizarre goings-on in the house were neither figments of the occupants' imaginations nor indications that they were collectively going a little mad.

Kelly now realized that the ghost had made its presence known to those who had lived in the house before them. And apparently nothing as minor as new tenants was about to squelch the spirit's mischievous behavior. In the coming months, Madeline did her ghostly best to keep things "hopping" in the haunted house during the daytime. At least these sessions were easily brushed aside; when the wraith was active at night, she wasn't as easy to ignore.

Perhaps feeling lonely or neglected in the quiet of night, Madeline would periodically turn the television set on—with its volume cranked to the highest possible setting. Other times, she'd concentrate her phantom powers on the stereo and turn it on, also with the volume blaring. Of course, these nocturnal pranks managed to startle everyone in the household into instant and often irritated consciousness of Madeline's existence.

The ghost was blamed— probably correctly—for light bulbs in the house never lasting a reasonable length of time. "They would always blow out," Kelly wrote, "yet no electrical problem was ever found."

Kelly reported that anytime she was in the house she always had the uneasy feeling that she was being watched. And although she was never able to determine why, she found "the living room to be especially spooky." Other signs of the haunting were not so consistent. Pockets of cold air, for example, were randomly sprinkled throughout the entire home.

Despite Madeline's aggressive haunting style, she allowed herself to be seen only once. Joan, who had been in a deep sleep one night, awoke to the sight of someone beside her bed. It appeared to be a lady with long, flowing, raven hair who was dressed all in white. Joan closed her eyes for a mere second, but when she looked again, the vision was gone.

Although Madeline was never seen by anyone else, her presence certainly didn't leave the house. Kelly and her extended family lived in that haunted North Bay home for two years. When they did move, their reasons were in no way connected to the ghost.

Since those years in the mid-1990s, the former occupants of the haunted house on Copeland Street have never again shared their days, or nights, with anyone other than flesh-and-blood beings. But they have noticed that the house in which they were treated to so much entertainment from beyond is for sale more frequently than are any of the neighbouring homes. Kelly, Dan, Joan, Sam and Brody are all quite sure they know the reason for this anomaly—Madeline.

Park Street Presence

Apartments can also be homes to ghosts. A small suite in a charming old building on Kingston's Park Street has a history of being haunted. Over the years, many tenants have reported that the ambience in this particular flat is decidedly sorrowful. A recent occupant, whom we'll call Carol, likely discovered the reason for this melancholy atmosphere when she saw the image of a ghost.

It was the middle of the night and Carol had been in bed sleeping for some time. She awoke suddenly for no particular reason. As she opened her eyes, she was shocked to see a clearly defined shadow in the doorway to her bedroom. It was a shadow of a man.

For her first few conscious seconds, the sleepy woman was terrified that someone had broken into her apartment. But when the image disappeared before her eyes, Carol realized that she had seen not a live person but a ghost. Perhaps this apparition was a visual confirmation of, or contribution to, the depressing atmosphere that always seemed to pervade the place.

Another night, Carol decided to stay up later than usual. She was quietly listening to some music when she was jolted from her reverie by the distinct sounds of someone knocking heavily on her door. No one could be calling on her at this time of night, she thought; perhaps this was another visit from the shadowy form.

Hesitantly, Carol opened the door. Before her stood two uniformed police officers with stern looks upon their faces. Some neighbours in the building had called them after hearing a gun being fired. The sound, they were sure, had

One of the residents of this apartment building saw the ghost long rumoured to haunt it.

come from her apartment. Yet Carol, who had been in the suite all evening, had not heard any noise at all.

The constables searched the flat, then the building, then the grounds. Finally, they probed the entire neighbourhood. They found nothing that might have indicated a gun had been shot anywhere in the district that night.

The odd occurrence, though, did offer a possible explanation for the Park Street presence. The sound of the gunshot might well have been the ghostly echo of a long-ago crime, and the image that awakened Carol might have been its victim, perhaps a resident of the suite. That theory would certainly explain not only the apparition but also the terrible feeling of sorrow that remained in the apartment. For everyone's sake—dead and alive—let's hope the sad soul has by now left the apartment and gone on to its final reward.

Scottish Spirit

The names used in this story are pseudonyms. The real names of everyone involved are in my files.

In the mid-1970s, Jack and Eileen Cook were offered the chance to move into a 150-year-old stone farmhouse in Pickering, a picturesque community on the shore of the St. Lawrence River. At the time, they were raising two little girls, so the opportunity seemed like a perfect fit. Little did they know it was also a welcome set-up for the home's long-standing resident ghost.

As the Cook family was preparing to move in, the soon-to-be-former occupants, the Bakers, were preparing to move out. On moving day, those preparations were interrupted by little Melissa Baker's screams. Mrs. Baker ran towards the child's bedroom, thinking the girl had experienced a nightmare. Much to her horror, she found smoke filling the house, wafting up the stairs to the children's bedrooms on the second storey.

Melissa was hysterical by the time her mother reached her, but not just because of the smoke. She had another reason for being upset. "Mommy," the child wailed, "somebody's on my bed. I felt him sit down." In panicked confusion, Mrs. Baker groped along the surface of her daughter's mattress. At exactly the place the child had indicated, there was an indentation, as though someone had been sitting there. Worse, that person must have left only moments before, because the spot was still warm to the touch.

To this day, no definitive explanation for the smoke has ever been found. None of the fireplaces were burning or even open, and there was no smoke in any other part of the house.

It wasn't until many years later, when the Cook family had lived through some strange encounters of its own, that the Bakers finally got a possible rationalization for the bizarre event that had occurred on moving day.

The Cooks happily settled into their new home. The only part of the house that Eileen Cook didn't like was the basement. My informant, Judy (Eileen's closest friend), explained that she didn't think Eileen "ever went into the basement. It was a creepy place with creaky stairs and a dirt floor. She just wasn't going down there."

No doubt the woman's aversion to the unpleasant cellar was made even worse by the footsteps she used to hear on those stairs—footsteps that occurred only when she was alone in the house.

Given the typical sensitivity of children, it wasn't long before Eileen and Jack's little girls also became aware that something about their home was unusual. They were never frightened by the phenomenon, but they did recognize and talk about it. Ghosts and haunted houses became a common topic during family discussions.

Judy recalled one time when she was visiting her friends and the children mentioned the resident wraith. "Being quite young, those little girls wanted to know what the ghost's name was. Eileen just said, 'Well, we don't know, but we can write him a note and ask him. We'll leave it on the fireplace.'" They did this and then waited a few days, but nothing happened. "I thought they had left the note to the ghost on the fireplace the whole time," Judy said, "but Eileen's husband told me that after a few days they threw it on a desk in an anteroom off the room where this fireplace was located."

This ordinary snowman had no facial features when this photo was taken, yet a face is visible in the picture.

And that desk is where Eileen found the message a full week later, but by this time it included a carefully written reply. "She was cleaning up," Judy remembered. "She picked up the note and [at the bottom of it] in this beautiful Old English script was written the name Percy. I absolutely guarantee that no one in the house had done that."

From that moment on, the Cook family members were able to address their invisible housemate by an accurate name. Some further investigation into the background of the property confirmed that the appellation was correct. The house had been built by "a Scotsman named Percy who immigrated here because his two young daughters were asthmatic," Judy explained. "He thought that the Canadian

Here the snowman seems to have developed an even more spirited expression.

climate would be better for them, but they didn't survive. Apparently his two girls died in that house."

As the months went by, the spirit seemed to grow stronger—strong enough to actually appear in photographs. "One of the pictures is of a snowman that the kids made out in the backyard," Judy described. "There were other children visiting that day; there were five little girls in all. They made a little step in front of the snowman and the girls sat on the step all around the snowman and had their pictures taken three times. When those pictures were developed, one showed the face of a man on the face of the snowman."

When Judy heard my gasp at this revelation, she stopped in her telling and acknowledged, "It gives you goosebumps, doesn't it? All they'd done was poke two holes for eyes, draw a little line for the mouth, and I think they stuck a stone or something on for a nose. But the picture actually shows a profile of a man's face superimposed on to the snowman's face. You could see his nose and his chin and that he was looking down at these little girls sitting in front of him."

And that was not the only photo of Percy. "Another picture is even more interesting, I think," Judy said. "The house is all stone, but the doors and windows were wood-trimmed. [The Cooks] were having those areas painted. The fellow who was painting was so enthralled with the architecture of this house that he went home and told his daughter about it. She was a photographer."

After checking with the Cooks, the painter's daughter began taking snapshots of the home. "When she had these pictures developed, she showed them to her dad and he spoke to my friend Eileen. He asked, 'Did this house ever belong to a Scotsman?' Eileen told him that, in fact, a Scotsman had built the house 150-odd years ago. The painter showed her a picture that his daughter had taken. In front of the house there were two big pine trees and between the trees was an image of a Scotsman with his kilt and tam on. He was just standing there in between those two pine trees. It was just absolutely incredible."

Jack and Eileen acknowledged that Percy was a very friendly ghost and that he always loved the girls. They believed it was Percy who had sat on the edge of Melissa's bed the day the Baker family was leaving the spirit's home. The ghost obviously had a special place in his heart for little girls.

But despite his devotion to the children, Percy sometimes carried his poltergeist-like pranks a little too far. The farmhouse he had built, and remained in to haunt, "had a beautiful master bedroom with a big bathroom that had an old claw-foot tub," Judy recalled. "Every night, [Eileen] used to take off her rings and put them in the medicine cabinet. She had three rings—her two and her mother's wedding ring, too.

"One morning [Eileen] got up and her rings were gone," Judy continued. "She couldn't figure this out at all, and she didn't say anything about the rings to anyone. Roughly three weeks went by. Her husband was down in the basement one day. He came up and asked Eileen, 'Did you lose your rings?' " The woman hesitated for only a moment before confessing that her rings had been missing for some time. 'Well, I found them in the crawl space down in the basement. They were on the dirt floor. The three of them were sitting there together.' "

At this point in the conversation, Judy reminded me that the basement "was a place Eileen had never, ever been. And I know her husband didn't take the rings down there, either. The little girls were far too small at the time; they couldn't even have reached the medicine cabinet. And besides, the rings disappeared when everyone in the house was sleeping. Those rings were gone for some three weeks."

Perhaps Percy realized that he'd caused concern, because he never played a practical joke again. But he certainly didn't leave the home either. As a matter of fact, those little girls grew to adulthood in a house with two adults and one ghost who loved them dearly.

I learned the details of this ghost story during a warm and friendly telephone conversation on a frosty winter morning. Judy generously spoke at length about Percy and his (after)life with her friend's family. Sadly, Eileen died in the mid-1990s, but Judy and her husband, Hank, have stayed such close friends with Jack that he was spending the winter with them.

"I'm telling you all of this for him, the husband of my deceased friend," Judy reported. "I wanted him to do it, but he said, 'No, I don't remember the stories the way Eileen would remember the stories.' "

One small postscript is needed to end this story. As Judy and I chatted, the long-distance telephone transmission was as clear as we've come to expect from sophisticated modern technology. Clear, that is, except for one prolonged and near-deafening blast of static that assaulted our ears. We both admitted to wondering if that might have been Percy eavesdropping. Perhaps he just wanted to make sure that we got his story right!

Stone House Illusion

As demonstrated by the previous story, Ontario's old stone houses are treasured pieces of the past. It's devastating when they're lost, not only to the owners but also to our remaining physical history. Therefore, many of these stately residences have been designated for preservation as heritage homes. They're all prime real estate investments, especially appealing to those with an appreciation for the past.

Jean wrote to tell me of one such dwelling in Ontario. Jean's daughter Jackie owned the property. The young woman lived there with her son, Michael, and a very noisy ghost. When Jackie's sister, Jennifer, came for a visit, the phantom really let its presence be known.

Jean explained that "after everyone had gone to bed at night, Jennifer was awakened by what she thought was Michael's heavy footsteps moving back and forth in the next room. She became annoyed because the sounds seemed to go on forever. Jennifer opened her door to go to his room and tell him to stop making such a racket."

The boy's aunt never got that far, though. When she looked out of her bedroom door, she saw a figure in a long white gown walking along the upstairs hallway. It didn't cross Jennifer's mind that anything out of the ordinary was happening; her sister had been wearing a long white gown at bedtime, and the image was heading toward Michael's room. The weary aunt simply assumed it was Michael's mother going in to settle the boy down.

Jennifer returned to her bed and, because it was now quiet in the house, quickly fell asleep. "In the morning," Jean wrote, "Jennifer asked Michael why he had made so much noise."

The youngster replied, "I thought it was you." Puzzled and perhaps wanting some confirmation of her suspicions, Jennifer then asked Jackie if she had gone to Michael's room to tell him to be quiet. The child's mother had no idea what her sister was talking about. She'd slept soundly right through the night. The ghost had been strong enough not only to keep both Jennifer and Michael awake but also to allow itself to be seen, yet Jackie had heard nothing of the commotion.

The apparition and the phantom noises were a one-time occurrence. The spirit may well have been living in the house with Michael and Jackie all along, but it only allowed itself to be detected that once. The mystery was never solved, but Jean acknowledged that the event "made for some interesting speculation."

Michael might simply have been receiving signals from the dimension that children seem to be able to tune into more easily than adults—the dimension from which some say ghosts communicate. And Jennifer, her mother wrote, is more "receptive to odd happenings" than are most adults.

Interestingly, Jean informed me that Jennifer now lives in London—England, not Ontario—and that she also owns a 600-year-old house in France, where both she and her mother have had two inexplicable encounters. I suppose it would be strange if a building of that age did *not* have some spirits moving about in it!

Time Warp or Haunting?

No one knows whether or not this is an actual ghost story. Legend states that the supernatural figure in the accounting was a witch, but Wicca is much more widely understood now than it was when the events occurred, and it is unlikely that the woman in this story was a witch. What we can be sure of is that the being in question is not an everyday person—she's definitely some sort of paranormal phenomenon.

A long time ago, in an unpretentious area of Windsor, an elderly woman named Mrs. Hallie lived alone in a home so small that it was often referred to as a cottage. Over the years, the woman's neighbours had many occasions to wonder about the sole occupant of the little doll's house. Despite the woman's frailty, her property was always well tended. The walks were shoveled in the winter and the gardens maintained in the summer.

Speculation grew about both the home and Mrs. Hallie. By September 1959, the interest—and the gossip that went with it—had spread beyond the community and made its way to two psychic investigators. These sensitive people were intrigued and made a special trip to the house.

When they started out on their endeavour, the two psychics had no intention of contacting Mrs. Hallie or asking to go into her home; they just wanted to walk past the place to see if they sensed anything out of the ordinary. But as they strolled along the sidewalk in front of the tiny cottage, Mrs. Hallie called out to them, inviting them inside.

"I know why you've come," the old lady informed the investigators. "My neighbours have been talking about me again, haven't they? Well, it's true what they say. I do have haunts that help me with the place. They won't show themselves to you, though, so if you want to learn more about the spooks, you'll have to speak to my neighbours."

It was clear to the two visitors that the woman's brief moment of hospitality was over. They thanked her for her time and courtesy, then backed out of the house and onto the sidewalk. As they retreated, they discussed their encounter. What bothered them both the most was that the inside of the house was spotlessly, unnaturally clean.

Somewhat hesitatingly, the psychics began at last to put one foot in front of another and make their way back to their own homes. But before their second step had been completed, they stopped in their tracks. They'd both heard a sound coming from Mrs. Hallie's house.

No one else was anywhere near the place, but something was very different about the front lawn. A moment later, one of the psychics pinpointed the difference: the pile of leaves that had neatly stood just to the right of the cottage's front door was gone. It had simply disappeared. Within mere minutes, a pile of leaves so large that it would take at least two people an hour's worth of effort to move had suddenly and inexplicably vanished. By now the psychics had seen far more than they had anticipated. They hurried in the direction of their own unhaunted homes.

Once the investigators recovered from the bizarre encounter of that afternoon, they set off on a ghost hunt again. This time they approached Mrs. Hallie's neighbours. Without much prompting, nearby residents described watching Mrs. Hallie fly or float out of her house and told of finding footsteps across fresh snow in her front yard. Footprints in snow aren't unusual—except that these marks seemed to start in the middle of the snow-covered lawn, then suddenly and mysteriously stop.

One neighbour must have developed more interest in these supernatural occurrences than Mrs. Hallie thought necessary. Not many days later, his house also showed signs of being haunted. "Furniture sometimes moved of its own accord across the room, right while we were watching," the neighbour reputed. "Sometimes dishes and cups jumped into the air right off the table and broke on the floor." These strange activities are often associated with the presence of a poltergeist.

Not all of the ghost's paranormal activity was designed for living beings to witness. For example, the entity usually turned on the water taps when no one was home so that no one was there was to notice that the house was flooding!

Near the end of September, the psychics who'd visited Mrs. Hallie earlier in the month returned to pay her another call. As they approached the house, they couldn't help noticing that the place looked very different. Instead of being neatly kept, the yard and the small home were in terrible need of repair. Both looked as though they'd been neglected for years, yet the two visitors knew that the place had been in immaculate shape only a few weeks earlier.

The investigators knocked on the front door, expecting Mrs. Hallie to answer. Much to their surprise, no one came to greet them. The door swung open on its own. The psychics called out but received no reply. A foul, musty odour wafted out through the door opening and unpleasantly assaulted their noses.

After taking a deep breath of fresh air and holding it, the psychics walked into the dark interior before them. Laces of cobwebs decorated every corner available, and it was clear that those cobwebs had been there for some time. Incredibly, they were dusty. How could this be?

The pair quickly made their way back outside. The sunshine on their faces was a relief, as was the sound of birds chirping. It had been completely quiet in the strange house, unnaturally so. The psychics stood staring at one another in disbelief, then decided that they would ask the neighbours if they knew what had happened to the enigmatic little cottage. The answers the men received certainly didn't bring them anything in the way of comfort.

When they weren't able to track down the neighbour in the house that had also been affected by a haunting, the investigators began knocking on other doors in the community. No one in any of the nearby homes had the faintest idea what the two were talking about. The tiny cottage had been in that dilapidated condition for ages, ever since the strange woman who had lived in it for so long had died—more than three decades earlier!

If that was the case, then who had the psychics seen when they had visited before? To whom had they spoken? Where was the neighbour whose house had been flooded after invisible hands turned on the water taps?

The explanation for this extremely unusual haunted house story might be a phenomenon known as *retrocognition*. Many of us are familiar with the term precognition as a description of the ability some people have to sense the future. The word retrocognition is not as commonly used, but encountering the experience itself is apparently as profoundly moving. Simply put, retrocognition occurs when a witness sees people or places as they existed many years earlier. The witness literally relives a part of the past.

Ghost story books are sprinkled with wonderful tales of retrocognition. For example, in the state of Washington (see my *Ghost Stories of Washington*, Lone Pine Publishing, 2000), a woman was walking down the stairs in a store when she was stopped in her tracks by a scene being played out in front of her. The basement of that store was, for that woman in that brief instant, decked out as it would have been 100 years earlier. She saw shoppers and store clerks all dressed in clothing from a long-ago era. Seconds later, the retrocognitive setting dissolved as mysteriously as it had been created and was replaced with the look and feel of the current day.

These visions of the past are not always a solitary experience. An example of a shared instance of retrocognition took place in Vancouver when a setting from the past appeared to a group of people who had gathered in a friend's living room. Part of the enigma involved a big, old-fashioned bed that suddenly became visible in a corner of the room where no bed had been earlier. When the retrocognitive sight disappeared from the partygoers' view, indentation marks remained on the carpet where the heavy bed had been seen.

In another well-known paranormal story, a fire department in rural central Alberta is frequently called to the scene of a burning house on an isolated lot. When the firefighters receive such a call, they know that the blaze being reported is one that occurred many years before when a fire burned to the ground the house that had once been on that lot.

The psychics who visited the little cottage in Windsor may, therefore, have encountered Mrs. Hallie's ghost enveloped in the continuing resonance of retrocognition.

Across Town

A house on another road in Windsor was also once home to some ghostly activity. The living occupants often woke to the sound of furniture being moved around in the basement. They were never able to find an earthly explanation for the noises.

The family's pet dog would occasionally bark madly at the living room window for no apparent reason. And once, when one of the daughters in the family came to the animal's side and followed its intense stare, she saw three human figures dressed in hooded robes on the front lawn. Moments later, the images disappeared.

Another daughter was haunted by a particularly gruesome recurring nightmare in which a woman covered in blood and holding a knife came up the basement stairs. The day the child was wide awake and watched that horrific scene supernaturally played out before her eyes was the day the family decided to move.

It is not known whether or not the haunting in that Isabelle Street house is still present, but fortunately for those two young girls, the spirits did not follow them to their new home.

Castle in the Woods

At what point does a series of coincidences cease to be a group of mere accidents of timing and become a clearly defined, predetermined path? Wherever that point might be, it seems that in researching the following story, I was led far beyond chance or happenstance toward a firm insistence that this unusual story be told.

In the mid-1990s, when I was beginning to collect material for my first Ontario-based book of ghost stories (*Ontario Ghost Stories*, Lone Pine Publishing, 1998), geotechnical engineer Steve Bartlett learned of my quest. (Coincidence number one, I think.) As Steve and I began corresponding, I discovered that he enjoys looking at history from unusual perspectives just as much as I do.

Beginning with that one common bond, Steve and I have become friends over the years. (Perhaps this chemistry between us is the second coincidence.) Our e-mail exchanges usually centre on one paranormal topic or another, but our discussions have also covered a variety of other subject matters.

A few days after I was asked to begin compiling stories for this book, Steve sent me an e-mail message. At that time, he probably didn't think his note would become an especially memorable one. The topics he covered in it were really quite typical of our usual range. He referred, in a somewhat off-hand manner, to an enigmatic experience he'd had as a youth.

When Steve typed those words, he had no way of knowing that *Ontario Ghost Stories, Volume II* had just become a work-in-progress or that his casual comment about an event that had taken place in the 1960s would become an important addition to the book. (Coincidence number three? I wonder. Perhaps you will be able to judge after reading this account.)

Even as a youngster, Steve was an open-minded, accepting person and he loved nothing more than being out-of-doors. In 1966, when he and his friend Pete were in their teens, the two set out on a camping expedition. During the first night of the trip, Steve dreamed of paddling in a canoe toward a log castle on a wilderness lakeshore. When he awakened the next day, the images that his subconscious had created were still fresh in his mind.

Although he was sure that such a log castle could not really exist, Steve told his friend about his bizarre vision. Much to the young dreamer's surprise, Pete responded by continuing the description of the castle. (Those coincidences just keep on coming, don't they?) As it turned out, Steve's remarkable dream had been a type of premonition—a forerunner, a very distinct kind of paranormal visitation. The log castle he had envisioned in the woods was, and still is, very much a reality. It had existed since Jimmy McOat single-handedly built the huge home in 1914.

Somehow, the magnificent Castle of White Otter Lake had "called out" to Steve Bartlett while he slept under the stars that night. Not surprisingly, this was a "call" the young man could not refuse. He and Pete soon set out on a quest to answer whatever it was that was drawing them to the extraordinary building.

Nearly 40 years later, Steve not only thought to tell me about the incident but was also able to turn up a postcard that he had purchased at the time of his visit. The caption on the card reads: "THE CASTLE—on remote White Otter Lake in Northwestern Ontario, has a romantic background.

There seems to be no question that Jimmy McOat's spirit has stayed in the log castle he built.

Built single-handedly by a young recluse from Scotland, it is a realization of his dream to own a Castle."

These two sentences are sufficient for a postcard description, but the castle's legacy deserves a much more detailed accounting. And the majestic building has received that description in the many brochures, books, poems, magazine articles, photographs and paintings that have been created to tell the tale of Jimmy McOat and his magnificent masterpiece.

The castle stands on the shores of White Otter Lake, south of Ignace in northwestern Ontario. Castle expert Dennis Smyk (along with many other local residents) has devoted hours of time and talent to preserving and displaying the tribute to determination.

In a brochure about the castle, Dennis wrote of "a log building, 28' by 38' [8.5 metres by 11.5 metres]." The place is "three storeys high, with a four-storey tower and a two-storey kitchen. It was built of red pine logs varying in diameter from 10" to 18" [25 centimetres to 46 centimetres] with some as large as 24" [61 centimetres]. Some of the logs weighed, when green, almost a ton. The 26 windows were transported, ready-made, from Ignace by canoe over 15 portages, a distance of about 20 miles [32 kilometres]."

These facts are amazing enough, but they become even more staggering when you remember that in the years between 1903 and 1914, Jimmy McOat, a physically small man, built the mammoth structure entirely on his own.

There are many versions of the legend about McOat and why he toiled in isolation to construct such a residence. The brief explanation on Steve Bartlett's old postcard is the most widely accepted rendition of this little piece of Ontario history. And perhaps it is the most truthful.

Another version has it that McOat built the castle for his true love, who then jilted him. Other interpretations are less romantic. One indicates that McOat for a time considered having the castle used "as a convalescent home for World War I soldiers." Another implies that when he was a youngster, someone told Jimmy McOat that he would not amount to anything but would die living in a shack. The rest of Jimmy's life would be a battle to prevent exactly that from happening.

Although it took him the better part of a decade to build the castle, Jimmy lived in the place for just four years. In the fall of 1918, at the age of 63, McOat drowned while fishing. Despite the comparatively short time he had to enjoy his masterpiece, the very essence of Jimmy McOat's being came to be imbued within the building.

Today, largely through the hard work of people who have cared deeply about preserving the architectural oddity, the castle remains standing as proudly as it did the day McOat mounted the last log. One of the forces at work on this preservation is the provincial government. Another is Jimmy McOat's tenacious spirit, for Steve Bartlett is certainly not the only person to whom the castle has called out.

Elinor Barr, a tireless worker for the castle's continuing preservation, kindly responded to the following, carefully worded inquiry. "Has it ever crossed anyone's mind that the guiding force behind the preservation efforts might be McOat's strong spirit?" I asked.

"Of course it has," the knowledgeable woman began. "Many people have felt Jimmy's presence at the castle. I have mentioned it in public on several occasions. Peter Elliott, who produced the film *The Castle of White Otter Lake*, credits Jimmy with keeping his movie camera safe during a water-spout that, among other things, lifted his canoe and threw it 30 feet [9 metres] across the beach."

Miss Barr went on to tell me that Jimmy McOat's "posthumous presence" in the castle contributes to the plot in Elizabeth Kouhi's novel for young adults, *Escape to White Otter Castle*. "Jimmy's presence has always been associated with the continued existence of his castle," she said. "The castle has been threatened many times…but it has survived. Something always turned up to save the structure from flooding, fire, vandalism, theft, weathering and the ravages of time."

Miss Barr added, "I like to think of the castle as a study in survival, usually at the last possible moment—a cliffhanger, if you will. I like to think of Jimmy as the play-ful presence who has arranged to keep his masterpiece safe over the years. I hope Jimmy sticks around for a long, long time."

Today, the castle is open to the public. With any luck, Dennis Smyk will be one of the guides on the day you visit. And if the "coincidences" keep on rolling, the long-deceased builder, Jimmy McOat, will be there, too.

Evil Entity Travels

Picture a quiet, neat residential street. Trees line the walks like soldiers guarding the idyllic setting, their leaf canopies shading the people who stop on the pavement to visit with one another. Two-storey brick houses sit back from the road, displaying large front porches with comfortable-looking fur-niture. Nothing unpleasant could possibly happen on such an inviting street, could it? Nothing paranormal, surely. Well, yes, it could. And it did, a long time ago on Pembroke Street in Toronto.

When the Parris family found a house for sale at a reason-able price, they considered themselves very fortunate. Good houses were in short supply in Toronto. The housing short-age made the Parrises treasure their real estate opportunity all the more. Until they discovered the home's history, that is.

Evidence of the haunting did not turn up right away. As a matter of fact, the family settled into their new digs easily and happily. They were therefore totally caught off guard when they awoke one morning to find that every piece of furniture on the main floor of their house had been moved.

Once the initial shock of finding their belongings scattered about had worn off, the family held an informal breakfast table meeting. Perhaps, one person suggested, some friends had come into the house in the night and moved everything around as a practical joke. Yes, the others agreed, that must have been what happened, although the theory didn't really make sense. Not only had the doors been locked, but it would have been completely impossible for anyone to accomplish the rearrangement in silence. None of the members of the household had heard any noise at all.

Still, the explanation was the only one any of the Parrises could come up with. So the somewhat unnerved little group decided to chalk the strange incident up to a prank, put all the furniture back where it belonged and do their best to forget what had occurred. Unfortunately, the entity in their pleasant little house clearly did not subscribe to such logic. And the next night it demonstrated its disapproval in a life-threatening way.

The Parris children had been asleep for some time and their parents had been in bed for an hour or so when Mrs. Parris awoke in a frenzy. She could feel a pair of hands circling her neck and their hold on her was tightening moment by moment. The woman's struggle awakened her husband, who immediately turned on the bedside lamp. He was horrified by the sight that met his eyes. His wife, her eyes as big as saucers, was gasping for air.

When she was finally able to speak, the woman told her husband what had happened. She knew it hadn't been him who had attacked her because she had been able to see him lying beside her even as the invisible hands were strangling her. The bedroom door was still closed. No one else was in the room or had been in the room. But the life-and-death struggle clearly hadn't been imagined; large finger marks could be seen laced around Mrs. Parris' neck.

While the pair assessed the situation and composed themselves, they became conscious of noises coming from the main floor of the house. At first they wondered if their children were downstairs. But as they listened more carefully, they realized that they were hearing the sounds of furniture being moved about.

Terrified that their lives were in peril, the Parris adults slipped out of their bedroom quietly and made their way down the stairs to investigate the source of the noise. At the doorway to the first room they reached, the truth hit them—literally. Some unseen force hit Mr. Parris in the chest, and the blow knocked him to the floor.

As Mr. Parris struggled to stand up, the hands that had already marked Mrs. Parris' neck found her again. Both adults fought for their lives against a force they could not see, then ran back up the stairs, picked up their children and fled from the house.

Upon hearing of the family's horrible plight, the neighbours closest to the Parrises' home came forward to provide some local history. There had been a good reason for the house being available, and an even better one for it being affordable: a terrible event had taken place in the building just a decade before.

The owners at that time had been an unhappy couple. The wife had a penchant for constantly rearranging furniture, to the point that her husband had no peace. Their bickering ended tragically when he strangled her one night as she lay sleeping. Since that time, no family had managed to live in the place without being bothered.

If the history of the house was working against the Parrises' peaceful existence, at least the future of the neighbourhood was working for them. Soon after that frightening evening, a builder approached the couple and asked if they'd like to sell their home to him. The people next door were ready to leave the area, and if this man could buy both houses, he would have enough land to build a small apartment building. Not surprisingly, the Parris family agreed immediately.

The haunted house was soon demolished. Workers constructed the apartment block without any misadventures and no tenants ever reported being disturbed by any ghosts, angry or otherwise. The furious phantom and the furniture rearranger had left. They had gone along with the house's building materials, which had become part of the hunting lodge of a business tycoon named Mr. Weisenbloom.

Mr. Weisenbloom thought the bricks and lumber he bought from the developer were a tremendous bargain, but the industrialist was getting tired of constantly finding the furniture in his recreation home rearranged. And he continued to be bothered right up to the moment that the ever-active ghosts either moved or knocked over a wood-burning stove and started a fire. Mr. and Mrs. Weisenbloom were alone in the lodge at the time. They fled with only their lives and their nightclothes.

The couple never returned to the haunted pile of bricks and charred timbers. By now, perhaps nature has broken down the wooden beams and grown around the cement blocks, once again incorporating the possessed materials into a peaceful, idyllic setting.

The Haunting of Hill House

The sleepy little town of Port Dover on the north shore of Lake Erie is the setting of a haunted "hill house" that's even spookier than Shirley Jackson's fictional creation in her novel of the same name. The paranormal story surrounding this buried home is purported to be factual.

The house in question is not a mansion set atop a hill, but a small, one-storey home built on a flat stretch of land. The hill came many years later when mounds of earth were shovelled all around the sides of the little dwelling. So much earth was moved against the outside walls of the residence that the place was completely buried.

More than one explanation has been offered for this strange landscaping. Some say the homeowner wanted total quiet. Others maintain that a commercial enterprise on the same piece of land wanted to hide the house. The actual reason might be entirely different, but we'll never know for sure. Those responsible for surrounding the tiny dwelling with a hill are no longer available for us to question.

Although the purpose of the earthwork is shrouded in mystery, the odd appearance that resulted from the burial is not. A casual passerby sees two ordinary doors—set into the sides of a hill. Above the doors are several small open areas where there were once windows. All around the orifices are thick grasses and other vegetation that camouflage the existence of the building.

Local legend has it that an elderly widow lived in the house. Despite the entreaties of those with her best interests at heart, the woman obstinately refused to move. Eventually, the stubborn old soul died, as forlorn in the place as she'd been when she lived. Some say her body lay in the building buried beneath the earth for many months before it was discovered. That's not necessarily true, but events of the following years did imply that the woman's spirit—every bit as uncooperative after death as it was in life—never left her peculiar home.

With foolish daring, children in the area began talking about exploring the hidden house. As time went by, their adventures took them closer and closer to the home before they would run off screaming in delighted fright. Access to the interior of the house was not a problem. Although the doors were padlocked, the windows were completely open. They'd lost their panes of glass years ago.

These open frames eventually became invitations to the bravest of the town's children. The first child with enough courage to poke her head in a window—and the nerve to talk about it afterwards—was 12-year-old Patsy. Her inspection of the interior lasted only seconds before she retreated in terror.

The little girl was sure that she had felt a cold wind blowing inside the house. That was frightening enough, because there seemed to be no reason for any air movement inside the darkened cavern. Worse, Patsy had also felt the brisk breeze quickly change direction; the child had felt as though the draft was somehow trying to pull her into the subterranean depths.

The girl pried her head out of the window opening and made a dash for safety. Safety at that moment was at the side of her 13-year-old sister, Heather. Heather had stayed back some distance as her braver younger sibling advanced towards the house.

Once Patsy's heart and pulse rates had returned to normal, the child tried to describe what she had seen and felt. It was only then that she realized that in addition to the sourceless wind, there had also been a shadow—a dark silhouette—in the house. The image had been present about a metre from the child's prying eyes.

Patsy and Heather quickly agreed that they had done enough exploring for one day. They spent the rest of that afternoon playing with their friends in the warm sunlight, thoughts of the hill house as far out of their minds as they could keep them. But not many days later, their curiosity again overrode their fears and the girls headed back to the sinister abode.

This time Patsy and Heather took their dog with them for protection. They also took tools to cut through the padlocks on the doors. Avoiding the windows, they reasoned, would allow them to enter the house without fear of falling or of being drawn inside against their will.

As the sisters approached the mound in the field, they were surprised to see that the doors to the house, which had been previously closed and locked, were standing open. Was this some sort of an evil invitation, they wondered? They stood paralyzed with fear, simply staring.

Moments later, Heather realized that the girls' dog was no longer between the two of them. She swung around and looked for the animal. Sure enough, there was the pet, a good 15 metres back, cowering in the long grass. Despite the sisters' repeated attempts to coax the dog toward them, he absolutely would not budge.

Determined to continue their approach, Patsy and Heather inched their way toward the house. Slowly, one baby step at a time, they crept up to the open door. At first they could see nothing inside, only blackness. But as they moved closer and closer, they were able to make out ordinary household objects in the decidedly extraordinary house. A dilapidated stove stood in the middle of the room. Furniture that had not been new for decades stood at odd angles around the lone appliance.

Each step brought the girls closer to finding out exactly what had long perplexed them—what was inside the house. Each step also took them farther away from their frightened dog, who was now yelping in fear. Steeling their resolve, Patsy and Heather stepped through the doorway. Seconds later, a thin watery beam of light appeared in a far corner of the buried room.

The sisters blinked and wondered momentarily if the light they saw existed only in their imaginations. Then a menacing hissing sound could be heard and they knew it was real. The noise became louder and louder, and it was somehow hateful. The two girls fled in terror.

It took several days for Patsy and Heather's nervous systems to return to normal. The girls realized that they'd had a close call with a sort of danger they did not understand.

As the sisters grew from little girls to young women, they often heard their schoolmates tell stories about a ghost in the hill house. They said nothing. They merely nodded knowingly.

It was fully a decade later before Patsy and Heather ever went anywhere near the terrifying, tomb-like house again. By that time, of course, they were older and wiser. Unfortunately, this increased age and wisdom did nothing to make the dead birds they found surrounding the place any less frightening.

The tiny corpses only confirmed for them how very lucky they had been to escape from the home unscathed.

2

Lake Lore

Ontario's many lakes and rivers have given the province some of its most beautiful geography. No wonder the waterfront is where so many have chosen to spend their afterlife.

Haunted Lighthouse

On a Saturday evening in February in the early 1960s three teenaged boys from a northeast Toronto suburb made their way to the Toronto harbour. There the high school students, who shall be known here as Alan, Eric and David, boarded a ferry for Toronto Island and began considerably more of an adventure than they'd ever imagined possible.

The trio had heard about a dance being held in the island's small residential neighbourhood. The youngsters were motivated to attend the event out of sheer boredom. It wasn't as if there weren't such functions in their own community—on the contrary, the boys were missing a party at their school that very night—it was just that the friends with whom they had grown up in suburbia were starting to seem dull.

The lads hoped that going to a social event in an area so unlike their own would provide an opportunity for them to make new friends with other teens from different backgrounds. Once they reached the island and the evening progressed, it was clear that their plan was working exceedingly well.

At first the boys were strangers to those gathered in the hall, but by the time the evening was over, they were new acquaintances exchanging phone numbers with potential friends. Unfortunately, being unused to the restrictions of island living, the youngsters managed to miss the last ferry back to the city. They were stranded until morning in this unfamiliar place.

Once they realized their dilemma and its implications, Eric, Alan and David began somewhat desperately discussing the possible arrangements they could make. For the first time in their lives, phoning one or more of their parents for a ride was not an option. They would have to call home to let everyone know they were all right, of course, but parental peace of mind was all their phone calls would accomplish. How and where they were going to spend the winter's night was completely up to them.

Luckily a chaperone standing nearby overheard the frantic young men's conversation. "I couldn't help hearing what you were saying," the woman said. "Don't be worried. You can spend the night at our house. You've been chatting with my kids off and on all evening, and they're having friends sleep over as it is. You're more than welcome to stay. Three more bodies won't make any difference at all."

Grateful and relieved, the boys enthusiastically accepted the kind invitation. Soon the newly formed group made its way along the darkened, snow-packed streets to a small bungalow several blocks away. "You fellas can grab blankets and make yourselves as comfortable as you can on the living room floor," their host suggested, and then she retired to her bedroom for the night.

Silence initially reigned among the seven youngsters in the living room. The visitors felt extremely out of place. They had wanted to make new friends, of course, but had no idea that they'd find themselves lying down beside them. The two brothers who were sharing their home also felt awkward. It seemed rude to start a conversation with their old friends that would exclude their other guests, but what could they talk about that everyone would be interested in? Finally, David spoke up.

"We sure found out how different things can be even in a place so close to home," he stated somewhat flatly.

"Guess that's true," came the reply from somewhere in the darkened room. "We'd probably find it just as different if we went where you live. We were all raised here, so we don't consider having to work our lives around the ferry schedule to be anything but normal."

Buoyed by the little bit of conversation that had started, Eric asked, "What else is different here?"

A chuckle broke out in the room before someone replied, "We wouldn't know, because to us it wouldn't be different."

After a second or two of silence, another boy, one of the island residents, spoke up. "Of course, we have our ghost," he said.

"This place is haunted?" the trio from the suburbs chorused.

"Yup. I've even seen the ghost and so have some of our neighbours."

Soon all seven teenagers were sitting up, hugging their knees and listening intently to the first true ghost story they had ever heard. "Tomorrow morning, before you catch the ferry home, we can show you where the ghost lives," the storyteller began. "It's at the Gibraltar Point Lighthouse on the southwest corner of the island. If you don't believe me, when we're there you can read about the ghost on the plaque that the city put up. Maybe you'll get to see the spirit for yourselves. He's been there for more than 150 years."

The boy explained that as early as the 1800s people realized that they would need a lighthouse on the island's Gibraltar Point, so one was built in 1805. A man named J. Rademuller was one of the first lighthouse keepers to be assigned there. Apparently the job either wasn't too time-consuming or didn't pay too well, because Rademuller had a profitable sideline going. He made and sold home brew. During the War of 1812, his best customers were the soldiers stationed on the island.

Unfortunately, Rademuller went missing one night and has never been seen since. Not alive, anyway.

The story goes that two intoxicated soldiers went to the lighthouse to buy beer, and Rademuller refused to sell it to them. There were rumours that the two men were guilty of killing Rademuller, but no charges were ever laid.

Many people presumed that the drunken soldiers sobered up quickly when they realized what they'd done and immediately buried Rademuller's lifeless body. Their plan obviously worked well enough because records indicate that the body wasn't unearthed until the 1890s. By then the ghost was already an accepted part of the local folklore.

The speaker concluded, "Even now people talk about seeing Rademuller's ghost. I know for a fact that I have, and the whole family next door saw him one evening when they were out for a stroll. And on foggy nights, phantom moans and ghostly footfalls can be heard coming from the empty lighthouse. Over the years, many different people have seen shadows that shouldn't be there, or inexplicable glowing mists around the lighthouse."

David, Eric and Alan had been listening to the story in rapt silence. Although the speaker seemed to be finished with the tale, they were not. "Why is the man's spirit still here?" one of them asked.

The reply came from a voice across the room. "Some say Rademuller's soul can't rest until his murderers are caught and punished. If that's so, he'll be haunting the island forever because those guilty soldiers are long dead themselves by now."

Next, the boys heard the familiar voice of the storyteller. "Other people seem to think that the man loved his job so much that he's chosen to continue living it into eternity. Whichever, the story's true—the island's haunted. We'll take you to see the lighthouse before you leave tomorrow, but for now we'd better try to get some sleep."

The three outsiders spent a restless night knowing that an ancient spirit roamed nearby. The next day, true to their word, the boys who called Toronto Island home took their new friends to see the plaque at the haunted lighthouse. It read: "This lighthouse, one of the earliest on the Great Lakes, was completed in 1805. The mysterious disappearance of its first keeper, J.P. Rademuller, in 1815, and the subsequent discovery nearby of part of a human skeleton, enhanced its reputation as a haunted building."

To say the trio was intrigued would be to grossly understate the case. David even thought that he saw a shadowy form ascending to the historic warning beacon. Within hours, the lads were once again back at their homes and their familiar suburban lives. But it was a very long time before they forgot the night that they went looking for new friends and found a ghost as well. Their supernatural adventure showed up in Eric's Language Arts essay, in Alan's science project, in David's Social Studies assignment, and in virtually all of their conversations for weeks to come.

I have chosen to tell the legendary Gibraltar Point Lighthouse ghost story from this perspective because David, Eric and Alan were classmates of mine. I was one of those boring people from whom they so successfully escaped on that February night.

After our friends' experience, Toronto Island became a popular place for we students to explore. As far as I know, none of the youngsters from my school ever saw the ghost, but Rademuller's unearthly spirit was certainly still there. We became quite sure of that fact a few years later when a Toronto newspaper reporter wrote an article about a night he had spent at the haunted lighthouse.

The scribe's intent in tackling the assignment had been to prove that there was nothing unusual about the island's popular historic site. Unfortunately for his comfortable skepticism, he had come away with strong indications to the contrary.

To have a firsthand idea of what the lighthouse looked like inside, the writer toured the place with a reporter's ever-attentive eye. All seemed to be well. Several hours later, perhaps bored by the lack of both human and spectral company, the man went back into the tower. He noticed that some of the interior walls had odd rub marks on them at about shoulder height. This was not something he could have missed on his first tour because the rubbing had caused plaster to flake off and fall to the floor. Having nothing else to do, the man swept up the mess and then went back outside.

Sometime later, the writer went into the lighthouse a third time. He was startled to see that more plaster had flaked off the walls, creating even more dust. But this time the fine powder looked as though someone had walked through it, for there were footprints leading up the staircase. Even that skeptical reporter had to finally admit that there was ethereal activity in the tower, for he knew as an absolute fact that no living person except for himself had been near the place since he'd been there.

If indeed J.P. Rademuller continues to wait for his murderers to be caught and punished before he rests, it's likely that the Gibraltar Point Lighthouse will be haunted by the unsatisfied spirit for a long time to come.

The Keeper and the Captain's Ghost

On October 22, 1881, the *Regina*, her holds fully loaded with paying cargo, set sail from the dock at Goderich on the eastern shore of Lake Huron. She never reached her intended destination. An unexpected squall blew up, dumping water over the craft's leaky decks.

The *Regina*'s captain, a man named Amos Tripp, was an experienced sailor. He knew the situation was serious, that his cargo—tons of salt—would absorb all the water that the bay would kick up. He realized that the structure could not stand up to the added weight and that the ship would sink. But unlike his crew, Tripp stubbornly believed that the old vessel could make it at least as far as the relative safety of a nearby sandbar.

It didn't. The hull split, letting the bay water pour into the *Regina*'s holds, sinking her instantly. The crew boarded and launched a lifeboat just in time to flee with their lives. But like the stuff of marine legends, Captain Tripp went down with the schooner. Some say Tripp's body was eventually washed ashore on Cove Island. Others maintain that the captain's remains were never found. Whatever the case, it is widely accepted that the man's ghost haunts the island's lighthouse.

Over the years, many of those tending the lighthouse reported that they shared their job with an invisible assistant. They claimed that when they set out to begin their daily chores around the place, they would often find the jobs completed. Wicks were trimmed. Brass, mirrors and lenses were polished. The situation was unusual and somewhat puzzling, but no one seemed to mind the helpful phantom company. All were sure the spirit was that of Captain Amos Tripp, and all were certain it was benevolent and protective.

Tripp's shadow was said to patrol the beach on stormy nights like the one that took his *Regina*—and his life. One especially appealing legend indicates that the ghost returned to the land of the living to enjoy an occasional evening of card playing with those who were lighthouse keepers at the time. While that tale is likely to be mere whimsy, a much more convincing anecdote exists regarding the spirit's spectral activities. The year this eerie phantom visitation took place was not recorded but, thankfully for those of us who love ghost lore, the essence of the incident was passed down.

One November night, the light in the lighthouse suddenly went out. Without its glow as a guide, many vessels and their crews would be in peril. Fortunately, the light flickered and came back to its full, lifesaving illumination after a few minutes.

The next day, an investigation was launched. The keeper admitted he had failed in his duties. The light had indeed gone dark, but he'd worked to immediately restore the warning beacon. Although it was certainly not acceptable that the keeper had allowed the lamp to go out, the man was credited for his quick thinking and skill that enabled him to repair the problem so quickly. He continued on at his post, probably with a very guilty conscience. Fully a decade later, he finally came clean about his role in what had happened that night—and his theory about the events.

Apparently the man was inexcusably absent from his post that winter evening. As a matter of fact, he was not anywhere on the island. At the time of the incident, he had not dared to tell that truth. He knew that if his horrendous negligence was discovered, he would lose his job and possibly have charges laid against him.

The man's neglect of his post fully explained why the light had gone out. But how then did it reignite? The irresponsible lighthouse keeper had an idea. He had long known that a ghostly presence resided on the island and that the entity haunted the lighthouse. He strongly suspected the spirit was that of Captain Amos Tripp. And he believed that on that stormy and potentially tragic night, Tripp's ghost had illuminated the light, knowing that if it didn't, other sailors' lives would be in danger.

Don't Go to the Light

A lighthouse that is dark when it should be lit creates a very treacherous situation. Equally dangerous is when any other light is lit along a shore and could be mistaken for a lighthouse and used as a navigational point.

The latter is exactly what happened during the stormy night of November 24, 1872. A kerosene lantern glowing outside a boardinghouse near Collingwood on Nottawasaga Bay was misidentified by a watchman aboard the *Mary Ward*. Eight sailors drowned as a result of the error.

The *Mary Ward*'s voyage was to have been routine, but as the craft made its way from Owen Sound to Collingwood, a severe storm hit. In a matter of minutes, visibility on the bay was reduced to almost nothing. The captain knew he'd have to make port as quickly as possible. When the sailor on lookout called out that he had spotted the Nottawasaga lighthouse, everyone on board was relieved. They knew they would be safely docked in no time.

Tragically, the entire group was wrong. The light the man had seen was not from the lighthouse at all. And the *Mary Ward* would not safely dock. Instead, the steamer lurched its way onto jagged rocks near the shore and split itself open.

With no time to waste, the captain launched a lifeboat with some of his best men aboard. He instructed them to make their way to Collingwood, where they could find help for the stranded and storm-battered lake steamer. They did so, but unfortunately the squat tug that set out on the rescue mission was not able to maneuver itself close enough. After considerable effort, the tug's crew gave up and sailed away.

The men remaining aboard the *Mary Ward* were devastated at the sight of their rescuers heading back to port without them. A mutinous group of eight launched a second lifeboat and headed out in the tug's wake. These men were never seen or heard from again, and their craft was never found.

When the storm abated, a better-equipped rescue party went out to where the *Mary Ward* was impaled. All of the men remaining on the vessel were rescued. The eight who deserted ship had made a deadly choice. Perhaps in their final moments they had realized their folly, for it seems their restless souls soon came back to earth.

For years, the boardinghouse with the kerosene lantern hanging outside of it was haunted by a gaggle of eight ghosts. These phantoms were widely presumed to be the souls of the men who perished on that stormy night. Until it was finally demolished, the angry spirits haunted the place that they apparently held responsible for their untimely deaths.

Ghostly Portents?

There are a great many superstitions of the sea. A vessel should never begin a voyage on Friday; rats fleeing from a ship indicate a craft's final journey; a woman aboard a schooner will bring bad luck. But the sighting of a phantom ship is generally accepted as the most dreaded event in sealore.

Phantom ships, or "Flying Dutchmen" as they are often called, are ghostly images of vessels that have already been lost at sea. In some cases, the spectres are seen only once—often just after the ship has gone down. In other cases, the images are seen time and time again over many decades. No matter what the pattern might be, the paranormal phenomenon is never considered a good omen. Death, it seems, follows its appearance.

Phantom ship encounters are among the best-documented paranormal events. There was once even a royal sighting when Prince George (later King George V) stood aboard HMS *Inconstant* and watched in awe as the clear image of a ship from the great beyond sailed into view.

John McPherson was well aware of the existence of phantom ships and the implications associated with them. McPherson worked for a fishery company located on Lake Superior. In August 1922, he was a passenger aboard the lake tug *Reliance*. As the working boat made its way through the fog, everyone on deck was surprised to see another vessel directly ahead. Their surprise turned to fear when they realized the ship they were seeing was the *Lambton*. The *Lambton* had sunk four months earlier. Clearly the sight before their eyes could not be of this earth. It must be a phantom ship—a harbinger of doom.

Fortunately, the *Reliance* completed its mission without anything untoward occurring. But John McPherson took the encounter to heart, and when he witnessed yet another phantom ship less than two months later, he knew that his days were numbered. McPherson must have been a philosophical sort of man who was ready to accept whatever hand fate would deal him, because he boarded the *Reliance* once again on December 15.

It was to be the tugboat's final trip. Roughly 100 kilometres north and west of Sault Ste. Marie (on Lake Superior, very close to the Michigan border), wind from a vicious storm picked up the ship and tossed it onto an island. The men on board were off the water but far from safe. They had no food or shelter, and the temperature was well below zero. All of those stranded knew that no one could survive long under such conditions.

After a great struggle, the captain of the *Reliance* and six of his sailors were able to launch a lifeboat. Amazingly, this group of seven made their way safely to the mainland. They were all still in peril, however, because the storm continued to rage and the men had a long hike ahead of them. But despite the odds being stacked decisively against them, at least they were still alive.

McPherson and two others who had been left behind with the beached ship tried to wait patiently to be rescued but soon began to panic. They were certain that the lifeboat had capsized and that the men who were to bring help had drowned. Their only hope of survival, they thought, was to launch the *Reliance*'s last lifeboat and try to make it to shore themselves.

The three had not been gone long when a rescue party, arranged by the captain and the six men who had headed out first, reached the island wreck. Those who had stayed with the destroyed craft were promptly shuttled to safety. They lived to tell of their adventure many, many times.

Neither John McPherson nor the two men with him were ever seen or heard from again. They may have drowned when the ferocious waves capsized their small vessel, or they may have made it to shore but frozen to death in the wilderness that stood between the rocky shoreline and the help they so desperately sought. By now, no one can ever know for sure. All that can be said with any certainty is that for John McPherson, the sightings of the phantom ships were indeed omens of death.

Supernatural Niagara Falls

Even today, with all the marvels that modern technology has brought us, the Seven Wonders of the World strike awe into the hearts and minds of those fortunate enough to visit them. Unfortunately, we must travel a very long way to see most of these amazing spectacles. One exception, of course, is the world-class site located right here in Ontario: Niagara Falls.

It is doubtful that anyone who has seen the falls will ever forget the experience. Standing beside 155 million litres of water as it crashes straight down from a height of 54 metres invokes every human sense. The mind has a difficult time accepting what the eyes are taking in, and the icy spray of the water sets off tactile responses. Mostly, though, it's the ears that are affected; no one can escape the noise created by Niagara Falls.

Visitors to Niagara Falls have seen a ghostly image in the mist.

Mystical stories have surrounded the falls since long before Europeans first laid awestruck eyes on the majestic sight. The name Niagara is from a First Nation's language and means "thunder of water." According to these people's oldest folklore, He-No (The Thunderer) is a supernatural being who lives under the falls. Legend has it that He-No rescued Lewlawala, a beautiful young maiden who had thrown herself over the falls to avoid having to marry a man she did not love. According to the legend, He-No took her to his cave where she has lived—in spirit at least—ever since.

Postcards bearing this phantom's likeness were a popular souvenir even 200 years ago! Over the intervening years, observant tourists have seen the ghostly image in the curtain of mist rising above the waterfall. By now, the ghost of

Lewlawala is frequently referred to simply as "The Maid of the Mist." She and her savior, He-No, continue to be constant supernatural presences at Niagara Falls.

Ghost Ships

The following phantom ship story involves the sighting of not just one ghostly vessel, but two. Fortunately, their inexplicable appearances do not seem to have been harbingers of doom. Perhaps they were more retrocognition events than forerunners; that is, historical reviews instead of warnings about impending disaster. The spectres were those of the *Hamilton* and the *Scourge*, ships that sank in Lake Ontario near the Niagara area during the War of 1812.

It wasn't until 1975, when a team of divers began exploring the area, that the actual crafts were seen again. In the years since they had gone down, the physical entities had lain, perfectly intact, on the lake bottom. But their ghosts had frequently been observed by sailors during the more than 150 intervening years.

All sightings brought consistent reports: the phantom ships were square-rigged vessels travelling under full sail with their guns at the ready. They were lit in a peculiar shade of yellow, and images of sailors could be seen clustered together on their decks. The manifestations lasted for a few moments before the phantom ships seemed to be effortlessly tossed about by an unseen force. Then the old warships once again sank beneath the waves, leaving only the cries of the drowning sailors behind.

It is likely that in this instance the destruction of the two vessels and all hands on board has scarred the psychic atmosphere sufficiently so that the tragedy is simply replayed over and over again, as though on an infinite spectral loop.

Animal Entities

The huge black dog paced the shoreline. Its menacing eyes glowed red, like coals from Hades. Sailors who saw the hideous animal froze in their tracks. They were not afraid that the vicious-looking beast would attack them; they were concerned because they knew all too well that the sight of the dog was a signal of death. Most ships never completed a voyage once the ugly cur had been spotted.

Nightwatchmen aboard lake-going vessels were often the first to spot the dreaded manifestation. To a man, they watched in horror as the dog's image made its way above the foredeck of the craft chosen for doom. The sight of the animal appearing somewhere on the ship was an even more serious omen.

As the *Mary Jane* left the dock at Port Colborne on Lake Erie, a lookout on the ship caught the sight of the dog walking across the schooner's deck. Shortly thereafter, the ship was becalmed. Shore workers noted the dog on board the stationary craft, but must have presumed that the animal was a pet and that the *Mary Jane*'s captain was simply waiting for some wind. Sometime later, those on the dock noted that the *Mary Jane* was no longer in sight.

It's doubtful that those witnesses would have been so calm about what they had seen if they'd known that the *Mary Jane* was gone for good. A crew aboard the *E.P. Door,* which also foundered that night, thought they might have spotted a ghostly image of the *Mary Jane,* but aside from that, neither the schooner nor her crew was ever sighted intact again. Pieces of the ship and her cargo eventually came to Lake Erie's surface, but they only served to prove that the evil phantom had struck again.

• • •

Unfortunately, the only man aboard the *T.G. Jenkins* who saw the black dog the night it crossed his ship's deck had long ago lost credibility with his shipmates. He was known to be a drinker, one whose tall tales became less and less believable with each sip of liquor he consumed. So when he reported that he'd seen a black dog cross the bow of the *Jenkins,* no one believed him. The ship's captain was so annoyed, in fact, that he left the sailor at the next port.

The dismissal must have been humiliating, even for a drunken sailor, but as fate would have it, the discharge saved the man's life. The *T.G. Jenkins* never made port, and the ship and her crew were never seen again.

• • •

A majestic-looking white steed galloped the shores of Yeo Island for so many years that people came to call the rocky outcropping in Georgian Bay "Horse Island." And for a while, there really was a horse on the island. The loyal animal had been shipwrecked there and was simply biding its time, waiting for its owner to come to its rescue.

Sadly, the horse was never rescued and eventually died. Its image, however, lived on. For many years the animal's ghost was seen by those who sailed near the island. The horse's soul apparently remained hopeful that its owner would return. Perhaps because the animal's spirit was still filled with hope, sightings of the steed's ghostly image never did portend disaster for the observers.

One Remains

Discovery Harbour, near Penetanguishene on Georgian Bay, may also be home to a ghost. The spirit of James Drury, a sailor whose earthly existence ended in a ship's galley on New Year's Eve in 1839, is rumoured to haunt one of the schooners built to replicate those that sailed the bay during the mid-1800s.

Visitors to the area enjoy the tours provided by interpreters wearing period costumes, and their experiences are reportedly enhanced by an additional guide—one of the supernatural variety. Staff and tourists alike have heard inexplicable noises and seen glasses mysteriously disappear from shelves.

Perhaps the eeriest indication of Drury's continuing presence aboard the vessel is the occasional indentation on a bunk. According to those who have seen the enigmatic depressions, it looks as though someone had been sitting on the bed, even though no living being has been anywhere near the cabin. When this happens, it is assumed that the soul of James Drury is eternally replaying his final night on earth.

3
Spirit
Snippets

*Some ghost stories are
little more than fragments,
but they are no less intriguing
for their brevity.*

Three's Company

Fourteen-year-old Bill Saunders was walking home with his younger sister one day when he witnessed a sight so strange that he remembered it clearly until he was a very old man. Bill was puzzled by what he saw, but I (and perhaps my biases are showing here) don't think his experience was all that mystifying. Frankly, I'm sure that a spirit of some sort or another was merely escorting the children safely home after they had spent a full and happy day in town at the circus.

"Home" to the Saunders children was a farmhouse off Richmond Road, in what was then rural Ottawa. The evening was bright, the familiar path lit by a full moon. Just as the children began the last and most isolated stage of their trek, Bill—for reasons that were unclear to him—turned around to look behind them. Long, distinct shadows trailed after the pair, but oddly, there weren't just two shadows as there should have been—there were *three* well-defined human silhouettes. It was as though a third person was walking between the brother and sister.

Bill said nothing to his sister, sensing that if she knew about the strange manifestation he had seen so clearly, the little girl would become frightened. As discreetly as he could, Bill began checking over his shoulder every few minutes. The phantom shape remained with the pair for about two kilometres, until the children were in sight of their house.

Once they were happily inside and had told their parents about the day's adventures at the circus, Bill's sister fell asleep. Only then did Bill reveal the unusual circumstances under which the children had made their way safely home. Mr. and Mrs. Saunders could not (or did not) offer any explanation for the bizarre occurrence. Bill went to bed pondering his memories of a wonderful day with a strange ending, and he never did get any sort of an rationalization for the shadowy apparition that walked between the children that evening.

Bill Saunders went to his grave wondering who or what might have caused that third shadow to trail along between the ones that he and his sister cast. If Bill ever guessed that it was a phantom, he certainly never said so.

That ghostly and protective visitation occurred in 1864 and was reported in the *Ottawa Citizen* on April 22, 1933.

Sobbing Sophia

The War of 1812 left behind its share of ghosts. Images of ships from that time still battle on the Niagara River, and the illusion of three British soldiers making their way back from a skirmish has engraved itself on the psychic landscape of Lundy's Lane. Even Canadian hero General Isaac Brock created a ghostly legacy—the spirit of his fiancée, Sophia Shaw.

When Brock was killed on October 13, 1812, in the battle of Queenston Heights, Sophia went into deep mourning. Those who knew the woman attested that she never recovered from the shock of losing her future husband. She died, alone and wretched, still sobbing for her beloved.

Sophia's mourning must have been profound, because even though the home in which she lived was destroyed during the war, the house that replaced it was said to be haunted by the phantom sounds of a woman sobbing. No earthly reason was ever discovered for this other-worldly phenomenon.

Photogenic Phantom

In October 2001, I was a part of a phone-in radio show. One of the callers, a woman from Ottawa, shared the following unique experience.

In 1986, the caller's family went on a daylong outing and decided to record the get-together on film. Everyone who brought a camera took an assortment of shots—carefully posed group pictures as well as more candid photos of individual family members.

The caller was among those taking pictures that day, and when she had her film developed, she was in for a big surprise. All the snapshots she'd taken turned out well—so well in fact that she decided to have additional prints made from the negatives. To make certain that she was duplicating only the pictures she wanted, the woman examined the negatives very carefully. Her attentiveness was well rewarded, because it seems she had taken a once-in-a-lifetime photograph.

Although the image hadn't shown up on any of the printed photos, the caller asserted that "there is a perfectly formed [image of a] little girl at the side of one of the negatives. I saw it. My daughter saw it. We couldn't believe it. My daughter has kept that negative ever since. That child's image didn't show up on the picture, only on the negative."

When I asked the woman if she had any idea who the little visitor might have been, she was evasive and answered by saying only that "she must have come back for the family photo. The extra image was that of a perfectly formed little girl wearing a white dress. I'd say she would have been about two-and-a-half years of age."

It is rare to be able to capture the earthly manifestation of an apparition on film. To have such a phenomenon so clearly detectable on a negative and yet not on the photograph is the classic puzzle wrapped in an enigma.

Home in Spirit

Another intriguing old ghost story comes from Sudbury. These events occurred on the evening of January 21, 1910, when Mary Travers was alone in her house.

Mary's husband, George, was away on a business trip and was not expected to return home for several days, so Mary was completely surprised when she heard the familiar sound of his footfalls approaching the front door. The delighted woman ran to greet her beloved, but her joy quickly turned to dismay. As the man entered the house, his hat brim still pulled low over his eyes, Mary could tell that all was not well. Something about George's demeanour was decidedly amiss.

"Are you all right?" the concerned woman inquired. As if in answer to her question, the man turned his face fully toward Mary. She began to shriek in horror. The features were definitely those of her beloved husband, but his visage was stark white—as white as the snow he had stomped off his boots and onto the mat.

Mary's screams attracted her nearest neighbours, who came running to see what the problem could be. In the seconds before they arrived, the image of George Travers completely vanished from the front hall.

Shortly thereafter, sad news made its way to Mary. George had been killed in a train wreck—a wreck that occurred at exactly the moment Mary had first heard and then seen her husband's manifestation make its way into their house.

Puzzling Plot

Laura R. wrote to inform me of a puzzling experience that she, her sister Linda and a friend named Carol had shared. At the time, Carol was visiting Laura and Linda's home in Dwight, a town Laura described as located "between Huntsville and Algonquin Park."

Carol had never seen the area, so Linda and Laura decided that a walking tour would be a good way to introduce her to the place. "We happened to walk past the local cemetery, which is a very old one," Laura recalled. "We took a walk in just to check out the headstones."

Like many people, these three ladies enjoyed the little snippets of the past that appeared on grave markers—at least the ones they could make out. Because of the age of the cemetery, very few inscriptions were easily decipherable.

Laura continued with her description of their outing by explaining, "We noticed one headstone that had started to drop into the ground. The actual plot had begun to sink." Despite the overall deterioration of that particular site, the trio was able to make out the name Emily on the grave marker. Because that was one of the few stones with legible words on it, they specifically remembered the plot and talked about it later.

Some days after Carol's visit had ended, Laura went back to the cemetery for the sole purpose of visiting Emily's resting place a second time. She went directly to the area where they had viewed the tombstone, but oddly, wasn't able to find the grave she'd come to see. Dismayed, Laura searched the entire cemetery, one she described as being "fairly small." Despite both the graveyard's modest size and Laura's thorough search of the entire region, she could not then, or at any time since, locate Emily's grave. It had disappeared.

Haunted graveyards are actually much less common than would be supposed, but a phantom grave is exceedingly rare!

Possessed Piano

As explained in the "Haunted Houses" chapter of this book, Emerson Haneman was raised next to an extremely haunted home on his parent's farm outside Ottawa. He also recalled a strange story about a piano that refused to leave its home!

During the Dirty '30s, very few people had much in the way of possessions. But one woman in the village of Numogate (which Mr. Haneman explained was on Highway 15 between Smith Falls and Carleton Place) owned a piano. Judging from what happened after the woman died, it seems safe to assume that the instrument had been her most prized possession.

When this woman passed away, Haneman explained, "her husband sold the house. All the rest of the furniture was moved out of their home, but the piano could only be taken as far as the door. There some force would push it back into the corner where it had stood for years. No matter how many men tried to move it, they could not get that piano out of the house."

What was even more disconcerting to the movers was the disembodied female voice that they heard crying out in response to their efforts. The men finally gave up trying to get the woman's beloved piano out of her former home.

Not long after that puzzling failure to perform something as straightforward as moving a musical instrument from one house to another, the almost-empty house burned to the ground. Of course, fires can have many origins and certainly don't have to be supernatural in origin, but Emerson Haneman recalls that there was something quite eerie about the aftermath of this fire. He explained, "The piano fell into the cellar and was barely burned."

With almost no house now remaining around it, getting the piano out of the old place should have been a simple task. But no one ever attempted to accomplish it. Instead, Emerson continued, "the cellar was filled in after the fire."

So the woman's ghost had her way in the end—the possessed piano never left the land that had once belonged to her.

Buried Beneath

Sometimes ghosts have to work to get our attention. That was certainly the case in this next story. The entity who haunted a small store in downtown Kingston might have been there for as long as a century before she was finally able to get a living being to acknowledge her presence. And that acknowledgement only came after considerable effort—by both the living and the dead.

In 1976, a photographer opened a studio in some retail space. He had not been in business very long when he recognized that something quite out of the ordinary was happening. The man spoke to his wife about the strange events and the two decided to take a Ouija board into the store to see if they could contact the spirit they suspected was there.

Through the board, Theresa Inace Beam identified herself. She explained that she had been murdered many years earlier. The murderer, a man named Napier, had disposed of her body without a proper burial in an attempt to conceal his crime. He had dug a pit in the unfinished cellar floor, dumped her remains into it and shoveled the disturbed dirt back into place.

Napier's acts of evil went undetected. He got away with the murder and went to his grave with his deadly secret intact. Only he—and Theresa's revenant—had ever known where to find the incriminating evidence. The deceased woman's spirit indicated to the photographer and his wife the exact spot in the basement where the body lay.

Theresa Beam might have lingered in frustration at the lack of justice that had followed her murder, but as it turned out, the ghost had a different reason for sticking around. As the photographer and his wife watched in fascination, the restless phantom told them the details of her misery.

Letter by letter, the ghost spelled out her haunting explanation on the Ouija board. In life the woman had been a practicing Catholic. Her soul simply could not be at peace until her mortal remains had received the Church's blessing and were laid to rest in a Catholic cemetery.

Recognizing this information as a plea from beyond, the photographer and his wife began investigating ways they could help the stranded spirit. They tried performing church-sanctioned rituals to free the spectre from her ties with the living, but clearly those weren't effective because the ghostly activity continued.

In desperation, the couple began to dig up the basement floor. When they still had not found anything even remotely resembling a skeleton after hours of labour, they decided to do some additional fact checking. They found out that their hope of discovering the body and then arranging for a proper burial was doomed from the start. Through document research, the couple discovered that the coordinates of the basement had changed since Theresa's time, so her directions to them concerning the location of her mortal remains were inaccurate.

Not long after their failed attempt to assist the dead, the photographer and his wife moved their business to another location, leaving poor Theresa Inace Beam's anguished spectre alone once again. Because there have been no reports to the contrary, it is likely accurate to presume that her ghost still haunts the place today—and probably always will.

Enigmatic Whistling

According to a column in the *Newmarket and Aurora Banner-Era*, the ghost in a Newmarket home responded very poorly when the living occupants of the house started to renovate the kitchen. There was no indication of whether the ghost was male or female, but it certainly was a strong spirit.

Salt and pepper shakers in the toilet might appeal to a 10-year-old boy's sense of humour but the family that was trying to live in this Gorham Street house was not impressed. Nor were they pleased to hear the ghost's admittedly accomplished whistling skills. Televisions, radios and stereos in their home would also turn on when they were least expected, and always at full volume.

Whoever the spirit was, he or she must have had mood swings, because the ghost is blamed for hitting the homeowner on the head *and* for cleaning up the mess after a bowl broke. But even those pesky antics paled when compared to the night that a ghostly voice was heard transmitting over the baby monitor!

Author Acknowledges Ghost

Even world famous, award-winning poet, essayist and novelist Margaret Atwood has lived in a haunted house! In the April 2002 edition of *Reader's Digest,* Atwood describes the ghost-inhabited residence as being a farmhouse "just north of Toronto." Ms. Atwood, her partner, her daughter and even occasional visitors have heard mysterious footfalls making their way up a staircase and then along a hallway at the top of the stairs.

A guest of Atwood's might have been psychically sensitive, because she either saw or in some other way perceived that the presence was a woman wearing a blue dress. The woman in blue might have been linked to a child who once lived in the farmhouse; the ghost seems to make her way along the upstairs hall towards a room that was once a nursery.

Margaret Atwood no longer lives in the house, but presumably the ghost still does.

Road Wraith

Many people have reported a bizarre sight on Sideroad 17 at Hawkesville, a little community just north and slightly west of Kitchener. The background to this paranormal observation is intriguing.

In the early 1900s, a family's home burned to the ground. The mother, father and all but one of the children were killed in the fire. The child who was saved, a six-year-old boy, was adopted and raised by a neighbouring family. Sadly, by the age of 47, the survivor knew his own death was imminent. He had only one final desire—that his remains be buried alongside the family members who had perished in the blaze.

For unrecorded reasons, the dying man's last wish was not carried out. His body was interred next to the relatives of the family who raised him. Clearly this was not his soul's craving, because inexplicable activity has been observed in the area over the years. Ghostly images, often described as "silhouettes," carry a coffin from the spot where the man was actually buried, across Sideroad 17, to the place where he had longed to be buried beside his birth family.

The man's desire to have his earthly remains lying beside those of the people to whom he was related was so strong that it created something of an endless loop of supernatural activity in the surrounding atmosphere. To this day, that final journey is played out only when people happen to be watching. Or perhaps it is always being played out but is only seen by the living when certain unknown conditions are just right.

Bald Apparition

His bald head makes this ghost in a home on Norfolk Street in Guelph readily recognizable. The flesh-and-blood folk who have seen him have also named him. They call him Jimmy. It's thought that in the last years of his life Jimmy lived in this home, and that he loved it so much that he returned to haunt the place after he died.

Jimmy's image has been seen on different occasions, but it's easiest to tell that the phantom is around by the sounds he makes. Footfalls echo from otherwise empty parts of the house when the ghost is on the prowl, and doors are heard to slam closed when no living person is near them.

A Headless Ghost

The city of Stratford, Ontario, has a long and colourful history. I was therefore not surprised to find that it has its share of ghosts. The story surrounding one of these phantoms is especially eerie.

Probably the only thing more startling than seeing the ghost of a deceased person is seeing a *portion* of the ghost of a deceased person—and a portion is all that is left of Henry Derry's spirit.

The man had been dead for some time when his coffin was discovered disinterred and floating down the Avon River in 1876. Authorities hauled the bobbing casket to the riverbank, pried it open and found Derry's body still resting there—minus his head. This gruesome find was extremely puzzling because the man's body had been intact when it was buried.

In due time, the grave robber, a medical student in need of a human head to study, was caught and punished. Derry's spirit was not to be dealt with quite so easily. It is said that his headless ghost haunts the Avon River to this day.

Ghost on the Links

Rumour persists that a prestigious golf course just west of metropolitan Toronto has always been home to a ghost. The land on which the course was laid once belonged to a religious order. One of the monks, it is said, has not left his abbey. His image has not only been seen but has also been heard, quietly reciting his prayers, apparently completely oblivious to the current-day activities surrounding him.

Cemetery Spectre

Fictional ghost stories are often set in cemeteries, but in reality most souls return to haunt settings that were familiar to them in life. That said, at least one exception to this generalization exists in southwestern Ontario.

The Belsyde Cemetery in Fergus, north of Guelph, is said to be haunted by a ghost playing melancholy songs on the bagpipes. The sad refrains are often heard at midnight. Legend has it that the deceased Scotsman's soul longs to return to his native Highlands.

Ghosts and graveyards seem to be eternally connected.

Irving

The town of Niagara-on-the-Lake may be the quintessential old Ontario town. Its tree-lined streets, big homes and cultural attractions make it an extremely appealing community.

Niagara-on-the-Lake was also a desirable spot during the 1800s, but for very different reasons. Back then it was a clever location for a fortress guarding against invasion from our neighbours to the south. It was the place where Fort George was built.

Today the fort is open to the public. Anyone interested can go on a tour of history—or a ghost tour. Kyle Upton began guiding ghost tours in the fortress in 1994. Right from the beginning, there was great interest from visitors hoping to experience a bit of very lively Canadian history.

Kyle kindly spoke with me at length while I was writing my first Ontario-based book of ghost stories (*Ontario Ghost Stories*, Lone Pine Publishing, 1998), and he shared many of the encounters that he and others had experienced in the fort after dark. Our conversation left me with no doubt at all that Fort George is a delightfully haunted place.

As do many people who work or live with ghosts, Kyle and his co-workers named some of the spirits remaining in the old buildings. That is how Irving, one of the most popular ghosts at the fort, came to have his appellation.

Irving spends most of his afterlife hours in either the barracks or blockhouse buildings. Tour guides at Fort George have heard heavy footsteps on the second storeys of these structures when there should not have been anyone on them. There are two stairways from the main floor of the barracks, and on one occasion, two guides ran up the stairs hoping to catch what they presumed was an intruder. Moments later, they were staring at each other across an empty space. No one was there. Then a shadow appeared. For a few seconds the featureless shape blocked the men's sight of one another as it made its way across the otherwise vacant room.

At closing time one night, another Fort George guide saw such a clear apparition of Irving that he began to speak to it, presuming it was a tourist who'd somehow been left behind by one of the tours. The man only realized that he'd seen and talked to something from out of this world when the figure vanished before his eyes.

But it's not just the staff at this historic site who have seen the ghosts—visitors have spotted the spooks as well. During a series of Halloween tours in 1996, many people reported seeing an old man hiding behind one of the beds in the barracks. They uniformly described the man as balding with a fringe of gray hair. No one meeting that description should have been anywhere near the bunks.

Although Fort George has many ghostly manifestations, Irving in particular has been blamed for occasionally slamming the blockhouse door. When an employee effectively dared Irving to close the door again, the ghost took the man up on his challenge.

Not content to let a phantom have the last act, the employee then propped the door open with a large, heavy bucket of sand. Seconds later, the door swung closed again—without so much as a grain of sand spilling onto the floor.

When the startled worker's head cleared sufficiently for him to notice, he realized that the still-full bucket of sand was now four metres from where he'd put it by the doorway. No one else was anywhere in the vicinity at the time.

Mirror, Mirror

Another haunting at Fort George does not seem to be related to anything military but is instead associated with an artifact in the office quarters. That artifact is a mirror that ties in well with the period being depicted, but is not original to the fort. Tourists and staff members alike have seen an image in the mirror—an image that makes no sense.

Everyone who has seen this strange presence tells of a woman with long, dark, curly hair wearing a white gown. The puzzling spirit may be growing in strength, for a child described the apparition in detail but was certain the ghost had been outside the mirror. No one has ever been able to come up with a rational, or even irrational, explanation for this haunting phenomenon.

4
Haunted Institutions

꩜

First we create the institutions
that are required to keep
our society functioning,
then we haunt them.

꩜

Eternally Doomed

Most of us make an effort to stay out of jails, so it seems rather odd that many souls choose to spend their entire afterlives haunting those institutions. And, this is not a new phenomenon.

On the front page of the January 12, 1884, edition of *Toronto World* (beside an article about a reception attended by Sir Casimir Gzowski, great-grandfather of the late broadcaster Peter Gzowski), a scribe gave a lengthy report about a ghost in a Hamilton jail. The history behind the haunting was grisly.

In 1876, Michael McConnell, a butcher in Hamilton, was convicted of killing a man named Nelson Mills. That same year, McConnell was hanged for his murderous deed. During the weeks between his trial and execution, McConnell was held in a high-security jail cell known as "the black hole."

According to the newspaper report written a full eight years later, McConnell's spirit returned to the area of his cell after his death. The scribe wrote, "McConnell's perturbed spirit will not rest quietly beneath the cold, cold ground and stubbornly persists in haunting the east yard, the east basement corridor [and the] western corridor where the 'black holes' or punishment cells are situated."

The journalist described the secluded cells as "small" and "provided with nothing." The locked bare rooms were places that even the most hardened criminals sought to avoid—and not just because they lacked comforts. "A man might naturally be presumed to have a horror of staying in a dark and comfortless cell, but prisoners dread to go not only for that reason but also because they declare they are haunted by the ghost of the man who was hanged on the wild March morning so many years ago," the story continued.

According to the story, the prisoners in 1884 were most emphatic about why they wanted to be kept anywhere but in the haunted section: "At night, they say the ghost flits from room to room and tramps up and down the long corridor with a ceaseless stride."

Such paranormal activity would have been scary enough in its own right, but McConnell's spectre became even stronger and more frightening each year on the anniversary of the hanging. A horrifying scene was recreated in and around the black hole corridor. Prisoners were said to "claim that the awful scene on the scaffold is all done over again, and a ghostly figure with a black cap on top falls through a trap door and dances for a minute in mid-air. Then all is still. The figure straightens out and death claims its own."

Even the usually hard-boiled jail guards were aware of the ghostly reality and its effect on prisoners. One turnkey of the jail said to a *Spectator* reporter that "the bravest and boldest prisoner would cry like a child and consent to undergo any punishment sooner than be put in one of the black holes with McConnell's ghost to keep him company. Big men who have never been accused of cowardice will shrink and shiver and pray not to be consigned there."

The haunting was taken so seriously that even higher-ups were notified about it. Predictably, the bureaucrats denied the possibility of such an occurrence in spite of such strong anecdotal evidence. They certainly didn't test the theory.

If any of those administrators had spent a night in that part of the jail, they probably would have been visited by the restless spirit—and they may have developed some empathy for the Hamilton convicts who were so terrified of the ghost.

Police Presence

In Guelph, a haunting in the police cells actually caused an officer to resign in January 1928. The erudite *Globe and Mail* newspaper advised its readers that a particularly active ghost, or perhaps ghosts, inhabited the southern Ontario town's headquarters of "the law-dispensing establishment." According to Chief Constable Alex Rae, conversations were often overheard emanating from the jail area of the station—even when no one was being held in any of the cells.

Woodstock Wraith

In Woodstock, a small city located halfway between London and Brantford, the old county courthouse and jail has been a proud landmark for over a century—and it's been haunted for at least that long. You see, the current courthouse building replaced an even older structure in 1888, and the wraith-in-residence there continued to prowl around the place as surely as he did the day he was hanged and buried on the grounds.

But how, you might ask, would anyone know this ghost's identity? The answer to that question is as clear as the apparition the prisoners in the old building reported seeing. They simply recognized the ghostly image of Thomas Cook, a convicted murderer who was executed on December 16, 1862. Further, workers unearthed a human skeleton in 1903. Documents revealed that the bones were found in the exact spot where Cook's mortal remains had been interred 41 years earlier.

It might have been hoped that the discovery would put an end to the hauntings, but such peace was apparently not destined to be. Thomas Cook's ghost, it seems, has never left the building. He made his spectral self known in a most irritating way during renovations in 1980. Materials and equipment that workers set out at the end of the day for use the next day inexplicably went missing, only to turn up later in a completely different area. It's certainly unlikely that any of the people working on the project would consistently inconvenience themselves or their colleagues in such a manner.

An old chimney stack was cleverly incorporated into a new elevator shaft. The entire area was sealed off except at the level where the new elevator car was being constructed, yet one or two tools that had been left in the lift would occasionally be found the next day in the building's boiler room.

After it was functional, this elevator would periodically take itself (or its invisible occupant) for rides from the top to the bottom of the building. The conveyance often stopped at the fourth floor—an area where Cook's presence was especially strongly felt.

Cook's ghost has also been seen in the dark, eerie tunnels that weave their way under the basement.

Haunted Hospitals

Hospitals, like jails, are institutions that most of us try to avoid. They're simply not very welcoming places, even when staffed with skilled and caring people. If you've ever been in a hospital that's empty, you'll know that such a building is an inherently spooky place.

Years ago, I had to deliver an envelope to one of the very few offices that remained occupied in the old University of Alberta Hospital just before it was demolished. I had no idea whether or not the place was haunted. I only knew that being in those empty, echoing corridors was a creepy experience and that I was awfully glad when I completed my errand and was back in the sunlight, walking (quickly!) to my car.

In October 2001, I spent several hours in a hospital that had been deserted for many years and was widely thought to be full of ghosts. I was there with the host and crew of a television show just a few days after they and a group of psychics had spent a night locked inside the old place. While I don't consider myself to be psychic, I have noticed that my sensitivity has increased considerably over the 10 years I've been researching and compiling true ghost stories. This heightened awareness was evident during my visit to the facility.

I knew nothing of what had gone on during the group's overnight stay, only that the television crew would be taking me through the former chronic care hospital and videotaping my reactions as we went. My experiences that morning were among the strangest of my career.

The first place we ventured into was the hospital's gymnasium. Much to the annoyance of the person operating the camera, I could barely walk into the room. The videographer had to change the angle of the shoot because I would not (or could not?) force myself to move away from the doorway so I could stand beside the man who was interviewing me.

I was later told that the psychics had seen a very angry presence sitting across the room from where I was standing. Interestingly, a former staff member confirmed that an extremely irate patient had once held himself hostage in that area.

While I found the deserted operating rooms and even the long-neglected morgue to be fascinating, those forlorn places had little effect on my emotions. I wonder if the crew was disappointed at my lack of reaction. If so, I must have made their day when we took the elevator to a floor of patients' rooms and my sensitivity kicked into overdrive.

I had been happily chatting with the crew and the show's host as we made our way through the corridors, but when I was directed into a particular room I was instantly overcome with sadness. Embarrassingly, I found myself fighting for composure. Although I'd been as cheerful as could be just seconds before, I was now very much afraid that I was going to cry. Only my pride, dignity and wide stubborn streak prevented me from embarrassing myself in front of my companions and the television camera.

Little did I know at the time that none of my escorts would have been surprised by such a tearful reaction. They were aware that the room to which they had taken me was haunted by the spirit of a woman who had died there while suffering from a deep depression. Once we moved back out of that room and away from the deceased's spectral sadness, I felt fine again. My experiences that day were so profound that it's unlikely I will ever forget them.

The following Toronto ghost story is also about a haunted building that used to be a chronic care facility. It's a tale that has a frightening twist to it. Some of the ghosts residing in the building are those of people who were psychiatric patients. Although the old building is now an educational institution, the spirits of those who were once so psychologically and emotionally ill have apparently not left the place.

John and Anne Spencer, in their book *The Encyclopedia of Ghosts and Spirits, Volume II*, relate the experiences of two curious students who decided to explore the cavernous old building. The pair heard someone whistling in an area of the place that they understood to be empty. They bravely turned to follow the whistling sound to its source, but the noise immediately stopped.

Thoroughly unnerved and determined to get out of the area, the two students headed for the nearest staircase. There they heard the whistling once again. This time the sound was accompanied by the sensation of cold air rushing past them, and that sensation was frightening enough to convince the duo to abandon their explorations once and for all.

Two members of a local ghost hunter society also had chilling encounters with invisible presences in this Toronto hospital. One member, a woman named Tamara, made a most interesting comment. She declared that she was constantly on edge while in the building and that she always worried that her perceptions would somehow skew and she would suddenly be exposed to retrocognition—seeing the place not as it existed at that time, but as it existed in its previous incarnation. The areas of the hospital in which she felt most uncomfortable were the tunnels. She was convinced that "something still uses them."

A security guard at the facility was also a member of that group of ghost lovers. Although he'd heard stories about spirits in the place, he'd never taken the tales seriously. It wasn't until he was assigned to work a graveyard shift that the man became convinced that the rumours he'd heard were true.

The security guard knew for a fact that no one else could possibly be in the building because the highly sensitive alarm system had been activated right up until the very second that he had turned it off. Despite this knowledge, the man recognized that the strange sound he heard coming from within a nearby room was very real.

The guard followed the noise until he came to a deserted chamber—one in which the revolving lid of a garbage can was, rather impossibly, turning around and around as though someone or something's hand had hit it hard. Could that have been the sound the guard had heard as he walked through the doorway of the building? Badly shaken, the man radioed a nearby colleague, advising him of a possible intruder in the place. Keeping in constant touch via their two-way radios, the pair of security guards scoured the premises but found nothing out of the ordinary.

Finally, feeling that they had done their job as well as they possibly could, the men prepared to leave the building. As they did, they became convinced that they were being closely scrutinized by a presence they could not see. The last sound either of them heard as they retreated from the strange place was a ghostly sigh.

It seems that while hospitals are places the living would prefer to avoid, the spirits of those who are already deceased tend to stay in them long after they've officially been discharged.

Last Visit

Greg Carter began his story by explaining to me that during the early 1990s he was working as a security officer at a hospital in London. At the time, the hospital administration was having electricians install safety cameras in and around the building. Over the weeks it took to complete the project, Greg enjoyed early morning interactions with one of the electricians, a man he has chosen to refer to only as Peter.

Greg wrote that "Peter was a jovial guy who worked in conjunction with the hospital security to install special outdoor cameras with zoom capability for parking lot monitoring. The zoom range of one camera in particular could focus out past the hospital property and onto a nearby traffic intersection, one that was well known for being the most dangerous in London."

Greg recalled his morning routine. "Peter would come in at 7:30 AM and work away at the camera system while frequently making jokes with me, the only other person in the room. Then, at 8 AM, the other electricians came on duty. One particular morning after about a week of this cycle of repetition, the camera, which was now fully functional, picked up a horrible accident at the traffic intersection at about 7:40 AM. A London police cruiser had run a red light and slammed into a small passenger car."

Greg responded immediately. "I reached for the 911 line, but was relieved to see an ambulance was already heading from our hospital to the site. Engrossed by what was happening on scene, and also busy responding to the dispatch morning calls, I never looked behind me."

Even though his attention was focused elsewhere, Greg was still aware that his pleasant workmate had arrived on the job. "I heard Peter enter the room as usual, and we had our normal jocular morning conversation. Close to 8 AM I heard Peter say something about being finished with what he was doing. Then I heard the voices of the [people on the] other shift arriving. The electricians arrived in a state of high emotion."

The reason for the workers' agitation was completely understandable, as was Greg's shocked reaction to their news: Peter had died in that accident at 7:40 AM.

The well-liked electrician, it seemed, had been so looking forward to his regular few minutes with Greg that even though his physical body was no longer capable of carrying out the routine, his soul took advantage of one last opportunity for a pleasant, early morning kibitz session.

Even all these years later, Greg Carter's sensitivity showed through in the words that he chose to conclude his description of this encounter: "Unfortunately, this is a true story."

It is also a persuasive and provocative bit of ghost lore.

Enigmatic Church Visitor

A similar ghost story took place at a church in Brockville where the minister once saw a ghost. He was not the only one to witness the apparition. The organist also saw the image. The form was so lifelike that the musician actually spoke to it. At the time he presumed he was speaking with the new pastor.

It was some time before either of the living learned that what they had encountered was the spirit of a parishioner who had died in the church and whose ghost was known to occasionally haunt the place.

School Spirit

Perhaps it is the intensity and variety of emotions experienced in large institutions that leaves the places psychically scarred. That theory would explain why an amazing number of educational buildings are haunted.

Today some official sources would just as soon avoid acknowledging that there are ghosts in schools, but in 1913 a report about a haunting in Uxbridge warranted a headline seven lines deep and two columns wide.

An unnamed journalist stated that "ghostly appearances and voices have been manifest in and around the school house." The article continued with the understandable report that "some of the children have been so frightened that they refused to go to school."

Details of whether it was the simple presence of a spirit that had the students scared or whether the entity's actions were particularly unnerving have been lost in the mists of time. What is known is that the more students stayed away from the building, the less the ghost made itself known. Poltergeists are often attracted by the energy of young people, and the description carried in the newspaper leaves little doubt that this was a classic poltergeist intrusion.

"The first agitation took place on May 17, when during a school session the lid of the stove suddenly flew across the room and clanked on the floor under the children's feet. Another time, the 'spirit' is said to have held a boy fast to the wall so that it took two of his companions to release him. Also, the combs were removed from a little girl's coiffure."

The writer continued, "The ghost is not silent and it speaks the language of the country. It has said frequently that it intends to visit other localities, which prophecy is heard gladly by the residents thereabouts."

Obviously, there was great concern about the spectre in the school, because supposed experts—or "persons competent to judge" what could be done to get rid of the ghost— were called in from as far away as 10 kilometres! School board trustees decided to deal with the haunting by appointing a committee to "look into the matter."

Today, most administrators would save themselves the trouble by simply denying that one of their schools was home to a ghost.

Museum Manifestation

Museums are particularly prone to attracting ghostly energies. In October 1992, newspapers all across the country carried a story supplied by the *Ottawa Citizen* about hauntings in that city's Canadian Museum of Nature.

At the time, the stately castle-like edifice had already been an Ottawa landmark for more than 80 years. Although we can't be entirely certain how long it had been haunted, there is little doubt that phantoms were in residence. Various people reported watching in awe as doors near them swung open and then closed again, even though no one could be seen close by.

Sourceless shadows also appeared in the museum. A security guard named Diane observed an amazingly detailed but only partially formed silhouette of a human shape. She later described the apparition as being transparent with a grey hue to it. The body was shapeless but the head and shoulders were well defined.

Another shadow was seen in a room displaying a dinosaur exhibit. This sighting was very different from the previous one. The witness described it as a huge undulating "wave of shadow." Despite thorough searches, no physical source was ever found for either of these hazes.

Entities have also been seen throughout the majestic structure. A female employee standing on the museum's fourth storey watched in awe as an apparition floated along before her. What upset the woman even more than the sighting was the way the phantom's eyes looked at her. The worker described them as "very piercing."

On that same floor, another employee was anticipating the museum doors opening when she was overcome by the notion that she was being watched. Turning around to inspect the room, the worker found she was alone. A second visual sweep revealed a human-like image in a nearby mirror. The manifestation was somewhat hazy but the woman was able to identify it as that of a tall man. She stood frozen in place as the misty shape moved out of the mirror, across the room and, much to her horror, passed through her temporarily paralyzed body. Moments later, the vision vanished.

Another very distinct sighting took place in the late 1980s, when the image of a young man appeared quite regularly to an employee. The two beings—one in this life, one in the afterlife—actually began to bond. To this day, the worker is sure that her ghostly visitor was trying to communicate with her each time he showed up. Unfortunately, the link between the two never became strong enough for an exchange of information.

Staff members also experienced the occasional sudden, full-bodied rush of goosebumps as they moved from one section of the building to another. Whoever these spirits were, their souls physically "reached out and touched" security guards at different times. Understandably, the people who were touched did not hang around long enough to learn if there would be any further communication. Without fail, they fled in terror and stayed away at least long enough to compose themselves.

One guard quit without explanation after having worked only one shift. He left his keys and walkie-talkie behind and took all his personal belongings with him. He never returned to the museum. Of course, one could argue that perhaps he had finally followed a childhood dream and run away to join

Some decidedly supernatural events have occurred in the beautiful Canadian Museum of Nature.

a circus. But those who knew of the situation were sure it was fear that drove the man out.

In the mid-1980s, a special exhibit about folklore and superstitions seemed to bring its own supernatural energy to the old gothic building. Displays of a broken mirror, a cracked sidewalk and a leaning ladder were set out along with an assortment of religious artifacts thought to be imbued with magical powers. Long-time museum employee Josy Diotte, who was the technical services director at the time, felt that the collection brought together "too much hocus-pocus and witchcraft in one place."

Perhaps as an acknowledgement to Diotte for having made such an observation, the eerie forces associated with the exhibit gave Josy a nod of the head—in the only way they could. A stone face mask that had been displayed in a locked glass case somehow managed to turn itself around 180 degrees between the time the museum closed one night and opened the next morning. No one who had a key to the showcase was in the building during that period.

Many staff members at the National Museum are aware that there is something special about their workplace. But it is the building's security guards and cleaners who are most cognizant of the inexplicable activities inside the old facility.

Certain areas of the spooky edifice are acknowledged by guards working the graveyard shift as being more difficult to patrol than others. The fourth floor on the west side of the imposing building is generally accepted as the most dreaded beat in the old Victoria Museum. The head of security for the museum is well aware that his workers will make almost any shift trade to avoid an assignment in this area—even if it involves giving up a day off work. The place is deemed to be that emotionally distressing.

Members of the janitorial staff sometimes toil away under less than ideal conditions. They report walking through localized, intense areas of either cold or heat. Thinking there is something wrong with the building's heating system, they invariably check the thermometers on the thermostats. Although they know for a fact they felt a difference in temperatures, the thermometers remain at proper settings.

Unnerving as those experiences might be, they are not the only bizarre occurrences the janitorial staff have to work around. Sometimes the cleaners are able to ignore the sounds of the building's elevators going up and down when they know for a fact there is no one in them. But when they finish cleaning one storey of the place, they use the elevators to move their supplies and equipment to the next level. When janitors lug the tools of their trade into the lift and push the button for the floor they wish to clean next, an invisible elevator operator occasionally thinks they should have a bit of a vertical tour first. At those times the elevator stops at several different floors, apparently quite randomly, before allowing the frightened worker to get off on the floor he or she needs to visit.

If that's not spooky enough, those same workers are often frustrated in their appointed cleaning rounds by the electrical cords on their vacuum cleaners becoming unplugged when there is no logical explanation for such a thing to happen.

Other phantom activity is so commonplace that it is almost unworthy of note. Alarms sound when there seems to be no cause for alarm. Electrically wired exit doors jam as though some force is holding them closed.

In 1989, a medium was called into the haunted museum. Whether or not the attempted exorcism she performed was officially sanctioned is unclear. What is clear is that the act was not completely successful. Signs of the hauntings continued as frequently after the ritual as they had before.

That constancy shouldn't be too surprising. A nearly 100-year-old building designed to resemble a gothic castle complete with twisting staircases and a basement full of mummies will likely never be entirely free of unintended and very lively supernatural exhibits.

Tag Troublemaker

Another of my favourite ways to learn of a ghost story is when a reader contacts my publisher and asks that his or her correspondence be forwarded on to me. That's how I came to know of the following supernatural encounter. The names have been changed slightly, and the name of the business where these ghostly events occurred will not be given, but beyond that the facts will be presented to you exactly as they were related to me.

Jeff, the man who contacted me, began by stating that he lives in Mississauga, where he works at a laser tag emporium, a place where laser tag games are played. Laser tag is a modern, high-tech, more challenging variation on the simple ages-old children's game of tag. Devotees describe it as "live action tag, hide and seek, cops and robbers, capture the flag and Buck Rogers, all rolled into one and enhanced with modern technology."

To play this form of entertainment, participants wear sophisticated laser transmitting and monitoring equipment. Players are armed with a laser "gun" and try to zap as many people as they can to rally up points. They also wear a special vest that receives and records harmless laser shots when another player "hits" it.

The best laser tag venues offer large, specially designed mazes that are divided into levels via elevating corridors. They add sensory input by means of pounding music, dramatic lighting and artificially produced mists. The laser game hall where Jeff works has a special additional enhancement, one not found in other halls. Jeff put it succinctly, I think, when he wrote, "There's a ghost in this building."

That awareness was more of an acknowledgement than a revelation, because the young man went on to admit, "We always knew there was a problem with our Tech Room, the room where we fix broken lights and battery pack problems. Things in there were always going missing. You would leave the room, come back and whatever you'd noticed missing would be there again. We always kidded around about there being little gnomes living in our Tech Room walls."

As an example, Jeff offered the following information. "One day, I was working back there fixing batteries. The doors have been known to close from time to time—but not to slam! The door slammed shut and the only things I could see in the darkness were the charging batteries for the packs." Fortunately, the door had not been locked, so Jeff was able to make a dash for freedom.

Understandably in need of companionship after such an unnerving event, Jeff sought out some old friends. After telling them of his encounter with an energy force he did not understand, his friends asked a reasonable question. If working there caused him so much anguish, why did he keep the job? Jeff had an unassailable answer. "I love working with kids and it's a whole lot of fun."

Jeff's workmates were also putting up with the supernatural experiences. "Everyone there knows the building is haunted," the young man stated. "It started with our assistant manager closing while alone one night. He was counting up the money when he heard a child crying. Thinking that we may have left a kid in the maze was terrifying enough, but the crying all of a sudden got louder. [The assistant manager] was kind of freaking out. It's almost as though the crying noise was coming from the speakers overhead. But when the crying turned into laughing, he bolted out of the building. He could barely tell us this story without freaking out again."

Jeff continued, "The next morning I was opening and nothing seemed out of the ordinary. Things were normal again for the next couple of weeks—until I was walking around the maze and found a little girl's T-shirt. It freaked me out...why would a kid take off her T-shirt? We would have noticed her coming out without her shirt. But when I told the story to my co-workers, they told me they had found other articles of girl's clothing in the maze as well."

The crying and laughing and the mysteriously appearing clothing marked the beginning of a great deal of ghostly activity in the laser tag hall. Jeff recalled, "Stuff started freaking us out, but we let it go. For example, I was alone in the maze one day when two out of three of the rows of overhead lights went off."

Because there was no apparent mechanical reason for this and other strange lighting malfunctions, the staff put the problems down to a ghost playing tricks. The ethereal being seemed very real to them, so they gave her a name. Marina, as the invisible spirit came to be known, rarely left the building after that. As Jeff says, "She's our friendly neighbourhood spirit."

If Marina's hijinks became too much, the workers simply let her know that what she was doing was causing a problem for them. For example, Jeff says that on more than one occasion, he's "yelled at Marina to stop goofing around" to calm himself down as much as the ghost.

There was one time when Jeff's admonishments didn't work. The ghost's response to being chastised was immediate and dramatic. "That's when all the lights went off. I took off, running into walls and smashing into things. As soon as I made it back to the front lobby, I saw my friend Rachel staring blankly at me."

As Jeff was enduring his unnerving encounter with Marina, Rachel was also witnessing bizarre occurrences that she couldn't explain. Machines in the front of the building "had gone crazy," seemingly functioning according to the will of an unseen hand.

Most recently, the presence from the past ensconced in the up-to-the-minute entertainment hall demonstrated to Jeff that she, too, could play the games. "The last thing that happened to me occurred while I was doing a change in batteries. A game pack started firing its laser at the wall all by itself. I actually videotaped it and showed it around. It was intense."

Jeff may love working with children and he may appreciate the fun involved in his job, but he's also sensibly unsure of matters he doesn't fully understand. "It's safe to say I only work the bare minimum number of hours a week there now," he wrote. "I hate being afraid of a silly, prankish girl."

Of course, the fact that this particular girl is actually a ghost goes a long way toward explaining Jeff's discomfort.

5
They
Returned

⌇

Why are there such things as ghosts?
Why do some souls return
but not others?
Why are some places haunted
while others are not?
Judging by the stories that follow,
the answers to those questions
are as varied as the ghosts themselves.

⌇

John's Not Gone

It takes a special sort of person to become a foster parent. Opening one's heart and home to children who are just passing through requires extreme generosity. Laura's parents were blessed with the extraordinary ability to extend warmth and protection to kids in need.

In the early 1970s, when Laura was a high school student in a community near Algonquin Park, she made friends with a neighbouring family. The family consisted of a mom, a dad, four girls and a boy named John. Laura had known the family for about five years when the mother unexpectedly passed away. From that point on, she recalled, "The kids were basically on their own."

The oldest child tried to keep the family together, but working, going to school and being responsible for raising teenagers eventually and understandably proved to be too much for her. So it was decided that John would be placed in a local boys' home. Laura's parents "talked about it and ended up being John's foster parents."

John lived with Laura's family for six years before a tragic motorcycle accident claimed his life. The young man's death hurt his foster family deeply. "It was a hard time for all of us because he had become one of our family. He was one of our siblings," Laura revealed. "After the accident, there were all kinds of court dates. It was very stressful. The person who caused the accident was eventually charged with vehicular manslaughter."

For a year after John's demise, Laura's family didn't have the heart to part with his belongings. His bedroom became a time capsule, preserved exactly as he'd left it. And yet, Laura explained that "there were a number of times when my parents, who were the only people living in our house at the time, would come home and notice that his bedroom light would be turned on when nobody had been in the house."

John's spirit apparently still lived in the residence at some level. Laura was to experience its presence very directly. "When my first marriage broke up, I moved back home with my parents and I stayed in John's room," she explained. "People could not believe that I had no problem sleeping in his bed, but as I got into bed, it was like I could feel John embracing me and I always had the most 'real' dreams there."

John's afterlife influence on Laura's present life became pervasive. "I never liked Neil Young's music," she said, "but he had been John's favourite singer." A small point maybe, except that during the time Laura was sleeping in what had been John's bedroom, she frequently noticed that her portable stereo mysteriously seemed to have Neil Young tapes loaded into it, ready to play. "I had the feeling that I was supposed to listen to them. Ever since then, I love Neil Young's music, the music John always listened to. Now I find it peaceful." Miraculously, John had found a way to reach out to Laura and give her the gift of peace.

He also reached out to his foster sister in a more tangible way. Laura recalled a time when her parents were away on a trip and she was alone in the family home. "Our poodle, Pierre, was lying at my feet while I read a book at the kitchen table. All of a sudden, Pierre started to growl and I could hear footsteps coming down the wooden stairs from the upstairs floor where the bedrooms are located. I didn't feel scared, but I felt as though somebody or something had walked right past me. It felt cool."

Laura wasn't the only one to sense John's presence. Another time, as Laura explains, "My mother was vacuuming and she felt somebody or something put both of their hands on her shoulders. It was almost a comforting gesture." Laura added that her father also had an encounter. He was "in the house by himself with the doors locked. He was having a bath at the time when he heard the back door open and somebody come up the back steps into the kitchen. Then a voice called to him by name, 'Hey, Earl!' My father quickly jumped out of the tub but there was nobody in the house."

Laura readily acknowledges that not everyone accepts her stories about John's spirit as being real and true. Fortunately, she doesn't require agreement from others because she knows for a fact in her heart and mind that these ghostly instances have occurred. The much-loved entity that was once John has never left the foster family's home.

A Special Goodbye

Kate Geisler is a valued employee of 100.5 EZ ROCK radio in North Bay. She also collects ghost lore.

Kate kindly wrote to me regarding some of the ghost stories she has compiled over the years. Kate shared the stories "Farmhouse Phantom" (p. 34) and "House Haunter" (p. 41). The following tale is one she considered especially appealing. I agree with her and perhaps you will, too. Kate began her tale by candidly admitting that this was a "story that actually touched my heart."

The informant, who identified herself only by the initials JP, told Kate of a reassuring encounter she had when her aunt died. The event occurred during the early 1990s in the Sturgeon Falls area on the north shore of Lake Nipissing.

All her life, JP had been extremely close to this particular aunt. So when the woman became seriously ill and was taken to a hospital in Sudbury, JP was devastated. The girl's uncle kindly drove down from Sudbury to Sturgeon Falls to pick her up and bring her to her aunt's side.

"JP spent the rest of the day with her aunt, talking and sharing memories," Kate wrote. "Finally, at about 1 AM, the family all went home. JP slept on the couch in the living room that night. During the early hours of the morning, JP was awakened by a strong wind coming from the window. The gust was so strong that it actually swept the curtains up."

At first JP was only mildly surprised. But when she woke up a bit more, "a strange thought occurred to her. It was January and the window was closed." Kate continued, "As the young woman's eyes focused on the window, she became aware of a figure standing nearby. It appeared to be glowing and was dressed in brilliant white clothing."

Understandably, JP was quite unnerved by what she was seeing. "As she tried to compose herself, JP looked [at the image] more closely. It was her gravely ill aunt, standing and smiling at her. But this vision of her aunt wasn't that of the frail woman JP had seen a few hours ago at the hospital."

The apparition was of the vibrant, beautiful person JP had remembered from years ago, and the smile was a great comfort to JP. The girl closed her eyes for a moment to see if she was dreaming. Sadly, the apparition was gone when she opened them. As JP lay on the couch trying to sort out what she had just seen, the telephone rang. It was the hospital calling to say that the family should come right away.

JP remembers glancing at her watch and noting that it had stopped—at 4:30 AM. It was now actually 4:45 AM. Although JP was terribly distracted by the urgent matter of getting to the hospital, she did recall thinking it was very strange that her watch had stopped. The battery that powered it, you see, was a new one.

As is often the case, the staff at the hospital had actually called just after the woman had died. The family was told that the aunt had passed away at 4:30 AM—exactly the time that JP's watch had stopped, and exactly the time she had witnessed the beautiful vision of her aunt.

JP had been granted a final visit from her beloved aunt in the vibrant form the woman would have wanted her niece to remember.

Historically Haunted

A former inn located just outside Ottawa was home to more than just the living. Before it was demolished in 1903, it was known for its "queer reputation." Mysterious sounds were heard for which there was no explanation, doors were seen opening and closing when no one was near them and doorknobs rattled for no apparent reason.

The building started off as the Richmond Arms Hotel. By the winter of 1879, the time when the following ghostly events began to occur, it was a residence owned by Thomas Dunbar and his family. The Dunbars had purchased the residence from the widow of Andrew Taylor. Shortly after moving in, they were advised that the woman had passed away.

Mrs. Taylor's lawyer asked Mr. Dunbar to distribute the belongings the previous proprietor had left on the property to the woman's relatives in Perth and Ottawa. In keeping with his reputation as a trustworthy citizen, Mr. Dunbar loaded the possessions onto his sleigh one snowy evening for delivery the very next day. Then he went to bed.

Mr. and Mrs. Dunbar both fell into a sound slumber shortly after retiring. They were suddenly awakened by knocks on their front door. Someone had banged loudly, not once but three distinct times. Mr. Dunbar quickly made his way to the entrance, but no one was there. Worse, there were no footprints in the snow. Mr. Dunbar was puzzled and somewhat annoyed by the episode; his wife was quite unnerved.

The next morning, after the pair had finished a hearty breakfast, Mr. Dunbar set out to accomplish his errand. Oddly, the man was unable to hitch his team of horses to the sleigh even though he was an experienced horseman. For some unaccountable reason, the animals were unusually skittish.

Just as Mr. Dunbar was leading the steeds back into their stalls, Mrs. Dunbar came out to beg her husband not to make the trip to deliver the possessions. For no reason she could fathom, she was experiencing an overwhelming sense of impending doom and was worried that something horrible would happen to her husband if he left that day. The man quickly agreed and the journey was postponed—for a much longer time than was initially intended. This extended delay was caused by Mrs. Dunbar's sudden and entirely unforeseen death.

Skeptics might call it a coincidence, but in a house already known to be haunted, mere "coincidence" seems to be an even stranger explanation for these events than a supernatural one. Perhaps it was the spirit of Mrs. Taylor who had knocked at the door the previous night, and perhaps that spirit had still been present on the property as Mr. Dunbar had tried to get ready to leave earlier that day. After all, paranormal entities are well known to "spook" horses—or almost any other animal for that matter. Perhaps Mrs. Taylor's phantom simply did not want another woman living in "her" house, especially one who would convince her husband not to deliver Mrs. Taylor's goods to her heirs.

Sadly, the lives of the remaining members of the Thomas Dunbar household were once again put on hold while they watched the man's 17-year-old daughter, Millie, deteriorate from the ravages of a terrible disease just a year later. Until the dying girl's very end, family and friends gathered in the house to offer her comfort.

One particular night, as the clock ticked its way toward midnight, Millie's brother, who had been lying on a couch near the girl, suddenly jumped to his feet shouting, "Who passed there?" Others tried to assure the distressed boy that no one had moved, but the lad was insistent. "Yes," he proclaimed, "somebody did—I saw a dark form!" A neighbour encouraged him to lie back down, but just a minute later he again jumped up and inquired, "Who was it that said, 'Three o'clock?' " Again those at the vigil tried to assure the boy that nothing out of the ordinary had happened.

Those gathered were apparently mistaken. Millie's brother must have been extremely close to his sister, for at exactly 3 AM the girl lost her battle for life. Could the shadow that the boy detected have been that of her soul crossing over? Perhaps. Or maybe it was the presence of a deceased relative coming back to the earthly realm to lead Millie to her final reward.

Midway Manifestation

Amusement parks, carnivals and midways are so much fun. They're places where we can escape the pressures of our everyday lives and feel free to act like children no matter what our ages. Such marvellous venues couldn't possibly be haunted. Or could they?

While compiling stories for my book *Ghost Stories of Hollywood* (Lone Pine Publishing, 2000) I was amazed to discover that Disneyland has developed its own folklore through the years—a folklore that includes ghosts! Although it no longer exists, the People Mover was once a star attraction within the Tomorrowland exhibits. It was also said to be haunted by the entity of a teenaged boy who had lost his life in a terrible accident aboard the ride. Staff and even some visitors were convinced the lad's spirit never left the spot where he died.

And that's not the only place where ghosts reside in the well-known park. Two other rides, the Matterhorn and It's a Small World, are also said to be eerily haunted, and inexplicable shapes have reportedly been seen on Tom Sawyer's Island as well.

Discovering these Disneyland ghost stories inspired me to unearth legends about hauntings in at least one other California amusement park and a park in Ohio. But what about locations closer to home? Surely we don't have ghosts in any of our Canadian theme parks? After all, the venues are all reasonably new places. Even so, it seems that we do have at least two haunted parks in this country. One of them is in Ontario.

While this was an undeniably gratifying bit of folklore for me to acquire, I was even more pleased to discover that a relative of mine had encountered the paranormal tale first-hand. John, as I shall call him, learned about the haunting while he worked at the park. He explained that the ride involved was a "a steel roller coaster with a train theme" and that it existed for less than five years. "The ride opened in 1981 and stayed open until mid-way through the 1985 season," he said. "I often wondered why it closed down. It wasn't until I worked there that I learned the truth."

John began his retelling of the ghostly legend by describing the routine followed by the well-run amusement park: "Every morning, before the park opens, maintenance crews inspect each and every ride. They check to make sure everything is technically and mechanically sound so that it is safe for the public. These inspections include preventative maintenance. If a ride fails the inspection, it does not open until the problem is fixed and another inspection has been successfully completed."

During one of these routine checks, a tragedy occurred. "On a summer morning in 1985, a young maintenance worker who had only been on the job for a week was [reputed to have been] killed while doing some work on the roller coaster. Details are sketchy, but I remember being told that a safety lock, which prevents the ride from operating while someone is working on it, malfunctioned or was accidentally turned off. Another worker started the ride."

For some reason, this second worker had no idea that his newly hired colleague was underneath the machinery at the time. Some people say the young man was crushed or decapitated by a train as it ran around the track. Others maintain that he bled to death after falling onto the jagged rocks below the ride.

"Whatever happened, the ride did not pass its safety inspection and it remained closed for the rest of the season pending an investigation," John confirmed. He added that, not surprisingly, "park management kept the details surrounding the accident quiet."

The killer coaster never reopened. Instead it was replaced with a similar ride that used the rails on which the previous train had travelled. John explained that "strange things began to happen and, as far as I know, still happen. Mechanically operated games situated below the new ride will frequently malfunction and stop suddenly while in use. At night, after the park closes, employees remaining on the site are often startled by bells, whistles and sirens that are mysteriously turned on. The stuffed animals that are given out as prizes have a habit of 'moving' from one spot to another, and the area has become a maintenance nightmare."

If you think that "nightmare" is an overstatement, consider the following freaky facts: "The lights in the building don't work properly. Power cuts are a regular occurrence. The main light switch doesn't work. You turn it on and off and nothing happens. The main power box is monitored daily for loose or cut wires and broken fuses. There's also a problem with the door that leads into the building. People have no problem getting in, but getting out can be a challenge—as though someone is pushing the door from the other side, trying to keep them inside."

Nothing seems to alleviate these strange problems. According to John, "Park maintenance crews are constantly fixing these problems. They have repaired the games, fixed the lights, oiled the door's hinges and even put new locks on the door, but nothing works. As soon as repairs are completed, things break down again. This cycle just keeps repeating, year after year. And the turnover in staff who work there is always high. Perhaps the young maintenance worker who was killed is trying to tell us something. Perhaps he wants to make sure that no one forgets what happened to him."

John concluded his chilling tale about a park millions of us have enjoyed visiting with these comments: "The park staff was certain there was some sort of supernatural phenomenon alive there. And, as far as I know, it is still there."

Wraith by the Water

The gentleman waited 30 years to go public with his first paranormal encounter, and when he did speak of it he gave his name only as W. Paul. Despite this reticence, his story of that ghostly incident—and the ones that followed—still managed to make headlines in the *Vancouver Sun* on August 24, 1931.

When Mr. Paul was a young man, he took a job in a remote Ontario lumber camp. At the time, the only way to reach the isolated post was by ferryboat. It was nighttime when the captain of the small craft docked and let Paul off at his new digs.

Not many moments later, the new arrival realized that the area was completely deserted and he couldn't possibly stay there overnight. He called out to the boat's captain that he needed to get back on board. As he spoke, a nearby movement caught his eye. He thought he'd been the only person to get off the ferry, but that apparently was not the case; not far from him on the dock was another man. "There are two of us here," he shouted.

The reply he received probably seemed very strange. "Oh, no, there's not," answered the captain, a man familiar with the area. "That's the ghost."

At the time, Paul paid little attention. He was just relieved to have caught the sailor's attention and he gratefully reboarded the small vessel. He was decidedly puzzled, though, to realize that the man he had seen on the dock was no longer anywhere to be seen.

Not surprisingly, the disappearing man became the topic of conversation between Paul and the captain. As he manoeuvred his ferry back out into the night, the captain assured his passenger that the man he'd seen had been a ghost—the remnants of a long-dead boatman who had plied the local waters for most of the years he was alive.

Paul was a skeptic and took the captain's information with a liberal pinch of salt. It made for an amusing story, perhaps an elaborate practical joke, but it certainly wasn't something to be taken seriously. After all, there was no such thing as ghosts—Paul knew that for a fact. Or at least, he thought he did. Unfortunately for his misplaced convictions, he soon found out that his lifelong skepticism was invalid.

Paul explained to reporter Doris S. Milligan that when he got back to the lumber camp for a lengthier stay, he discovered that the ghost was a well-accepted member of the community. "We saw him lots, sometimes quite close," Paul began, before describing the wraith as being a "big, handsome, well-dressed man" and adding that he and some workmates once watched as the apparition walked "down into the water as though it was going down steps."

If that observation did not prove to Paul that the image was not human, then what came next must have. Certain lumber camp workers thought that shooting guns directly at the ghost was great sport. They liked watching the bullets go through the lifelike form. That sight should have been more than enough to shake anyone's skepticism.

Paul initially wasn't frightened on the one day when he thinks the spirit actually meant to do him harm. Paul saw the ghost running toward him, but he had grown so used to sightings that he thought little of it. Then he suddenly realized that the image had a different, menacing look about him. Paralyzed with fear, Paul stood stock still as the long-dead boatman "passed right through him," leaving a wake of "strange wind." After this incident, Paul was so afraid of the ghost—a reality he'd scoffed at just months before—that he quit his job.

Paul was not the only man to remember the logging camp spirit. Staff at the *Vancouver Sun* confirmed his story with another man who'd been employed at that haunted lumber camp in one of Ontario's forests.

It is unlikely that Mr. W. Paul is still alive today, but it is reasonable to presume that he went to his grave with his altered beliefs intact. He was quoted as saying that those paranormal encounters left him a changed man, that his skepticism had been replaced by a hard-won knowledge that a spirit could survive a body's death.

In other words, Mr. Paul had begun to believe in ghosts.

Sharon's Friend Sharon

When Sharon Tapp first contacted me, she indicated that few people call her by her real name. Most use her long-standing nickname—Smiley. This knowledge made her true ghost story much easier to understand because, you see, the ethereal presence in the following account is also named Sharon. Throughout this poignant tale, I shall refer to my correspondent as Smiley and to her tragically deceased friend as Sharon.

Smiley began her note to me by saying that as a child and a young woman she generally "found it easier to relate to the opposite sex." But she added that she always had a few extremely close female friends whom she cherished with all her heart. She explained that when she was in her early 20s she "was fortunate to meet and become almost soul sisters with another female who shared the first name of Sharon. I lived in the Kanata region, just outside Ottawa; she lived in Ottawa."

This geographical separation meant that the young women didn't see each other day in and day out. But according to Smiley, their times together were "almost magical. Thinking back, I now realize that at first, subconsciously, I found the intensity of our relationship almost alarming. It was amazing how close we had become in such a short time."

The two girls enjoyed similar interests. "Music was a pleasure of life that we both loved immensely," Smiley wrote, "with the soundtrack from the movie *Flashdance* being a special favourite. Sharon and I shared not only good times but also helped each other through bad times. Our conversations were long and often deep. We covered a huge range of topics. We often discussed life after death and decided that when the time came for either of us to pass on, even if we'd had time to say 'goodbye' to one another, we would still come back briefly to say a final 'goodbye.' "

Having set a foreboding stage on which to present her paranormal encounter, Smiley carried on with her story. "Tragically, Sharon was involved in a terrible car crash," she wrote. "She suffered numerous internal and brain injuries and never did recover from the coma she was in. Three days later, she passed on."

If there was any kind of a blessing to be had from this tragic situation, it was that Sharon's doctor advised "that had she survived, it would have been in a vegetative state. Her brain injuries were intense. So fate was kind to let her slip away without feeling any pain."

For a while afterward Smiley did not live up to her nick-name. She was in shock and she retreated far away from the rest of the world. She listened to music day and night. Then came the day of Sharon's burial.

"I had a terrible time trying to prepare myself mentally," Smiley remembered. "As I waited to catch a ride to the funeral with Sharon's boyfriend, Mike, I turned on a song from the soundtrack of the movie *Flashdance*. Its melody seemed to take on a life of its own. As the music was swirling in my head, so was Sharon's and my relationship, right from the beginning of it through to the end. Just as Mike's car pulled up, the song ended, as did my dreamy state of memo-ries, but only ever so gently. I realized only then that I had the strength to carry on."

Smiley did the best she could to get over her grief, at least enough to keep functioning. She moved to a different house and tried to get out to see people. Then one weekend something strange happened. "I was visiting my sister in town…and arrived back home rather late that night. As I approached my driveway, I noticed that in the middle of each of the three upper windows of my home, the ones that face the road, there was a single, roundish orange light or glow. I slammed on the brakes very hard. The car came to a screech-ing halt."

Smiley was instantly terrified. What could possibly pro-duce orbs of light in a house that should have been empty and dark? Understandably, her first reaction was to flee. "I quickly turned my car around and raced back along the road, with every intention of returning to my sister's home and calling the police from there," she recalled. But as her initial fright began to abate, the urge to defend her property grew strong.

"I wasn't sure what was going on," Smiley admitted, "but it was my home and I was going to protect it. As foolish as it may seem today, I headed back to my home. To do what? I didn't have a clue. I raced down my driveway at a speed that I wouldn't attempt again. I was flicking my high beams on and off. I realized my fear was creeping back, but this time it seemed to bring some unknown source of energy with it. I ran to the door, unlocked it, turned on the kitchen light. I started yelling. I think I was saying words, but it's not clear to me today exactly what those words were."

Once she was in her home, Smiley tried to determine who or what had caused the eerie lights in the windows. "I went from room to room, turning on lights and leaving them on. I kept yelling, but the house was empty." Smiley says that she "tried over and over again to figure out what could have caused those lights in the windows, but no possible reasons ever came to mind." She couldn't see the orbs from inside the house, and she wasn't even sure if they had still been there when she'd returned to the house after fleeing.

"To this day, I can't remember if the round orange lights were still in the three upper windows as I raced down the driveway," she wrote. "I do remember having to concentrate as I sped along on the dirt driveway. It was winding and dipped down into a ravine before leveling off again back up at the house."

Smiley continued to describe the events as they unfolded. "The next day, after a sleepless but uneventful night, I went through my routine of getting ready for work. One of the things I do is make the bed before heading up to my shower. Before I leave the bedroom, I always glance backwards for one last check to see that things are okay."

No doubt Smiley was relieved to be able to focus on something as normal as preparing for work. Unfortunately for her peace of mind, when she finished her shower and walked back into the bedroom, she noticed something very small but still decidedly strange. "A small portion of the top corner of my quilt had been folded down as if someone was getting the bed ready for sleep," she recalled.

Smiley was understandably taken aback. She stood and stared only briefly, wondering how she could have missed that corner. Then, being a pragmatic sort, she continued to get ready for work, even though she had "a funny feeling inside."

Nothing out of the ordinary occurred during Smiley's workday and nothing strange happened that night. But the next morning, after her shower, Smiley again encountered something that caused her heart to pound.

"I came back down the stairs a little slower than usual, this time with a building feeling of nervousness," she wrote. "I peeked around the corner into my bedroom and saw that the corner of the quilt was folded down." Smiley was truly terrified now. Something was definitely in her house, something that seemed to be invisible.

"Now the chills were everywhere on my body. I was shivering uncontrollably. I stood frozen to the spot in front of the bed and stuttered out loud to myself to 'calm down, just calm down, there has to be an explanation for this!' " Desperately trying to regain her composure, Smiley stood stock-still. "I struggled to clear my head and all of a sudden it hit me. Sharon. It has to be Sharon!" Believing that it was the spirit of her dearly beloved friend helped Smiley to realize that this was an extraordinary encounter but not one that she needed to fear.

"Somehow I managed to will myself to sit on the end of the bed. I started talking and talking and talking and talking. I talked about our time spent together, about the accident and how I wished I could somehow have helped her. I talked about how I hoped she was content and happy, how I hoped so much that she would be waiting for me on the other side so that we could continue to be friends forever."

The passage of years has slightly dulled Smiley's memory of the details of that amazing morning, but her recollection of the emotions she felt is as strong as ever. "After quite a bit of time, I left my home…late for work but feeling very calm. The nervous, anxious feelings had left. The tightness in my stomach had also disappeared and my heart was beating normally, back in the spot where it belonged. As a matter of fact, I remember feeling lighter and happier than I had felt in a long time."

Just as the two friends had promised one another they would, Sharon had come back for a final goodbye. Smiley concluded the story of her encounter by stating that although she did not see an image of her deceased friend, the other woman's "spirit was definitely there." And that visitation has had a long-lasting effect on Smiley. She told me, "I still talk to Sharon from time to time during good times and bad about this and that."

There is something of a postscript to this story. Smiley said that "the fearful and nervous feelings are gone, but when I speak about that visitation the chills and shivers still capture me."

6
The
Spirit's
Inn

~

Hotels, motels, inns, hostels and
other temporary accommodations are all essentially homes
away from homes. It is therefore not much of a surprise
to discover that many of them are haunted.

~

Where Are They?

Staying at the haunted Bayview Hotel in Sault Ste. Marie might be a problem these days. I tried as many ways as I could think of to make contact with a person there, but had no luck. The place just doesn't seem to exist anymore. That shouldn't be too surprising; the building would be well over a century old by now. What is surprising—delightfully surprising for our purposes—is that a lot of information is still to be found about the ghost who once haunted the property.

The spirit was said to be that of a youngster who had been suffering from ill health. Perhaps in keeping with the thinking of the day, the child was kept cloistered—in the attic of the hotel. Never having had a chance to experience a normal childhood in life, this little spirit seemed intent on spending his or her afterlife playing tricks on every available adult.

The little ghost's favourite prank was to take people's possessions. Nothing of substantial financial value ever went missing, but small items that people required in their day-to-day lives often disappeared for no earthly reason—only to reappear, equally mysteriously, sometime later. This must have been particularly annoying to the staff at the Bayview Hotel, who were simply trying to do their jobs under less than ideal conditions.

Now that the hotel is apparently gone, it's interesting to speculate what might have happened to the mischievous little wraith who haunted the place for so many years. One can only hope that the child's spirit is now enjoying the freedom it was denied during life.

Haunted Inn

Ontario's Muskoka region boasts some of the most beautiful geography in the world. Dense forests shelter wildlife, fresh-water fish abound in crystal clear lakes, and idyllic rivers meander through it all. Right in the heart of this gorgeous setting, mere steps from the dramatic Bracebridge Falls, lies the quaint little town of Bracebridge.

In the late 1800s, William Mahaffy purchased a huge home in this pristine area. Since then and until quite recently, the mansion has changed hands and uses many times. Finding potential buyers with sufficient resources to keep such a large residence operating was not easy. As a result, the place has occasionally stood empty and become rundown.

During those years, rumours inevitably circulated about the impressive structure. Just for the fun of scaring themselves and their friends, local children decreed the house was haunted. Many years later, those same youngsters were quite surprised when one of the building's owners, a Mrs. Allchins, acknowledged that she could often hear phantom noises throughout its halls.

Today, people come from all over the world to stay in the historic residence, now called the Inn at the Falls. Management and staff at the inn take great pride in their well-deserved reputation for offering old-fashioned hospitality. Bob, Charlie and Sarah also extend their warm, hospitable greetings to visitors, even though they've been dead for many years.

The three ghosts who happily haunt the Inn at the Falls are such an accepted part of the charming hostelry that their presences are noted not only on the menus but also on the hotel's website. Bob, it seems, is usually in the kitchen. He's treated with great fondness by the staff, except when he carries his stunts too far and makes a pest of himself.

Bob's spirit is a strong one. He has been credited with tossing pots and pans across the room. It's presumed that this kitchen ghost does not tolerate crankiness, for he gave someone in a very bad mood a firm shove when no one else was anywhere near the man. Bob's connection to the inn during his life is not known, but it's obvious that he's felt a strong connection to the place ever since his death.

Sarah's association with the building is also unknown, but many people have seen a part of her ghost. She has long brown hair and wears a white dress. Sometimes her image is only seen from the shoulders up and at least once her image tried to communicate with the living by saying "hello." Sarah generally stays in the dining room.

According to the information printed on the menus at the Inn at the Falls, Charlie haunts the upstairs corridors. He, like the other spirits here, is a friendly ghost who tends to keep his own counsel.

The manifestation of a pregnant woman is seen and felt in the hallway just outside room 105. This poignant image may be the spirit of a lady who owned the inn with her husband for a time during the 1930s. The woman fell down the stairs during the final weeks of her pregnancy, and both she and the child were killed in the accident.

This ghost's enigmatic energy is strong. Guests have seen her clearly enough that they have presumed she was a living person and expressed concern for her well-being. As well, guests and staff alike have heard sobbing punctuated by

The Inn at the Falls is haunted by spirits reluctant to leave the beauty of Ontario's cottage country.

phantom footfalls making their way down the hallway. One visitor even overheard snippets of a ghostly conversation between the long-deceased mother-to-be and an invisible man.

William Mahaffy's spectre has also been seen in his former home. He's easy to recognize thanks to a portrait of him that's still hanging in his former home. This haunting is not too surprising given that Mahaffy loved his home very much. What makes it a little unusual is that William actually died in England. His soul must have journeyed across the Atlantic Ocean to spend its afterlife in Bracebridge.

Mahaffy's ghost cannot be confused with a living person because it doesn't so much walk as float about 15 centimetres above the floor.

Another former occupant who has chosen to stay on at the charming inn is Jackie Nivens. Jackie, her husband and her mother-in-law ran the place in the 1970s, when it was known as Holiday House. In 1983, years after Jackie's premature death, Cathy Morrow, the office manager at the inn, saw the image of a casually dressed woman approximately 40 years of age. Seconds later, the apparition vanished before her eyes.

Over her years with the inn, Cathy detected a pattern to the ghostly activities in the building. She noticed that early mornings and late nights were the busiest hours for supernatural activity, with the times in between being quieter.

These benign descriptions of the hotel's ghosts were confirmed by a psychic named Geraldine, who once held a séance in the inn. After entering a trance-like state, the psychically sensitive woman had little do to. Even the lights in the room dimmed by themselves.

Geraldine recognized many of the spirits known to haunt the building, but was somewhat surprised by the number of delightfully happy children's spectres she was able to detect. Perhaps those little guys account for the reports of ashtrays flying off tables and across rooms, clothing coming out of closets and small articles going missing. These items usually turn up sometime later inside haunted room 105, where yet another apparition spends her eternity sitting in a chair at the window. Those who've seen her say she appears to be looking for someone.

One of the most interesting observations about the almost magical qualities of the Inn at the Falls came from a one-time partner in its operation who claimed, "If this place does not like you, your stay will be short." Such a comment promotes a theory that the spirits are happy with the Inn at the Falls, and the soul of this extraordinary heritage building enjoys its current incarnation as much as the guests do.

Ghostly Guests

The Grand Opera House on Adelaide Street in downtown Toronto was demolished in 1928, but it remains an important component in the province's list of ghostly legends.

Ambrose Small owned the palatial Opera House from 1903 until his mysterious disappearance in December 1919. Since then, neither he nor his corpse has ever been seen. The man's ghost, however, is still observed at the Grand Theatre in London, Ontario, another venue in what was once Small's chain of entertainment investments (see the first volume of my *Ontario Ghost Stories*, Lone Pine Publishing, 1998).

Long before Small was associated in any way with Toronto's Grand Opera House, the theatre was already connected with another, very different haunting. This earlier ghost story began when Shakespeare's *Macbeth* was performed on the stage of the Grand. *Macbeth* features many elements of the supernatural, such as ghosts, apparitions, and witches with their predictions of the future and incantations over a boiling cauldron. The play revolves around themes of murder and death and powerful emotions of guilt, anguish and other torments to the soul.

These supernatural elements and forceful themes might at least partly explain why profound, deeply felt superstitions about the play have developed throughout the theatrical community. Actors, producers, stage hands, and anyone else involved in bringing *Macbeth* to audiences accept as a fact that an accident will occur during the play's run. They are also convinced that if they speak the title of the play, bad luck will befall not only the speaker but all concerned. As a result, anyone involved with the production will only make reference to "the Scottish play."

Despite all of these terrible portents, the opening night at the Grand (Friday, November 28, 1879) went so well that the cast decided to celebrate at the nearby Queen's Hotel. As they rejoiced, they had no way of knowing that the witches' cauldron continued to burn and bubble on the theatre's stage. Hours later, the elegant interior of the Grand Opera House was reduced to ashes. Only the exterior shell of the building remained.

Once again, *Macbeth* had wrought its fury. The play was successfully produced and performed, yes, but only for a single night. It would take additional investments of thousands of dollars and hundreds of hours before anything could be produced on that stage again.

The celebrants must have been devastated. What should have been the pinnacle of many acting careers was consumed by the voracious flames. There was nothing the actors could do to rescue their dreams or even their roles. The impact of the fiery event on at least one member of the cast appears to have been so permanent that it not only lasted her lifetime but also continued long into her afterlife.

The Queen's Hotel was demolished in 1927 to make room for the Royal York Hotel, which opened its doors in 1929. Legend has it that a revenant dressed in a gown from the Victorian era has occasionally been seen in this enormous landmark hotel. She might be a spirit tied to that opening night celebration of *Macbeth* at the Queen's Hotel long ago. After all, on her plane the old hotel may still exist and the party may still be going on.

A completely different legend surrounds the ghost of a man. His image, dressed in a smoking jacket, has appeared on an eighth-floor corridor in the Royal York. This man's identity during his life is not known. Nevertheless, his after-life existence is apparently generally accepted as being real.

Neither ghost has ever troubled anyone. As a matter of fact, the spirits seem as unaware of their current surroundings as they are of each other. According to historian and author David Macfarlane, the existence of the ghosts at the Royal York only contributed to the hotel's inclusion with other hotels of world-renown. In the book *Castles of the North*, Mr. Macfarlane notes that the hauntings meant that Toronto "had a hotel that had ghosts, as all great hotels do." (For more stories of this kind, please see Jo-Anne Christensen's *Haunted Hotels* and my own *Haunted Theaters*, both Ghost House Books, 2002.)

A ghost story lover can only respond positively upon learning of hauntings being given such proud and valued recognition.

Manifestations
in the Mynah Bird

Many years ago, I spent a portion of a New Year's Eve in the Mynah Bird Coffee House in Toronto's Yorkville area. It was in those days a hippie hangout—pretty exotic stuff for a kid from the 'burbs. Had I known at the time that it was haunted, I probably would have taken away a different impression of the place. As it was, I only remember the café as being big, noisy, crowded and smoky.

Like any other fad, the hippie "scene," as the vernacular of the day would have it, did not last forever. By the time the 1970s approached, most of those who'd called the Mynah Bird their second home had moved on to other phases of their lives. Management soon realized that they would have to change the theme of the place if they wanted to stay viable. So they did; strippers and their very different audiences replaced the earth mothers and peace lovers who had once read and listened to poetry at 144 Yorkville Avenue.

Although most of middle-class Toronto had no fondness for the hippie movement or those who subscribed to it, the ghost in the building was apparently fine with the counter-culture philosophies. It was the shift in demographics that came with the transition from a coffeehouse to a strip club that seemed to offend the resident spirit.

The displeased phantom began to make his presence known with typical ghostly tricks. Unfortunately, he didn't succeed in drawing much attention to himself through antics as easy to ignore as causing lights to go and off, even when such a thing was least expected.

The best guess is that the ghost was a man. When interfering with things electrical failed to attract the attention of the living, he become bolder. The strippers, not women prone to being faint of heart, began to tell the club's owner that they felt very uncomfortable in one particular dressing room. Upon hearing their comments, the proprietor knew that something serious was afoot. And he was right. The haunting had begun in earnest.

Heavy pieces of furniture would move about when no one was near them. Once, legend has it, chairs were thrown across a room by a powerful but invisible force. The musicians who accompanied the women's bumping and grinding complained that their instruments had moved, even though they'd just put them down a few minutes before. Nothing ever disappeared for a prolonged period of time, so theft was certainly not implicated.

Before long, everyone had given up denying the obvious. They realized the building was haunted. That acceptance proved to be a good thing, too, for it wasn't long before a disembodied male voice was heard by a gathering of female employees. Not only was the ghost gaining strength, the increased energy seemed to be motivated by anger. The ghost hated what was going on in his earthly home.

Strippers felt an antagonistic presence standing right beside them—too close beside them for their comfort, given the invisible being's negative aura. Any of the dancers who encountered this spectre knew immediately that he heartily disapproved of what they were doing.

Research into the history of the building indicated that the most haunted part of the strip joint was located where an artist had once rented a studio. Only one woman reported actually seeing the ghost, but her description of a grey-haired man with a beard matched the description of the artist who had worked in the space.

Whether the entity was the ghost of the artist or not, he certainly became an accepted, if discomfiting, presence in the place. It also seems likely the spirit wasn't alone on his plane, because people would frequently report detecting pockets of air heavy with the fragrance of a woman's perfume. The olfactory signs were definitely those of a ghost because they were not scents that anyone living carried with them, but rather smells that were detected as a person walked past a particular spot.

By now, both the hippies and the strippers are long gone. Perhaps the ghost is, too, for the building standing at that address today is a new one and doesn't seem to be the sort of place where a ghost might feel at home.

Or perhaps he's still there but he just hasn't become annoyed yet.

"Good Night, Harry!"

Ron Gostlin wrote to me about the ghostly encounters he had experienced while operating a haunted bar and night-club in an old resort on the shore of beautiful Lake of Bays near Huntsville. He began by describing a bit of the building's history.

"Around the 1920s, Pinegrove Inn was being operated as a year-round hotel," Ron explained. "A gentleman named Harry Corbett and his wife, Helen, owned the place. The inn was heated with a coal furnace and one of Harry's many duties was to keep the furnace stoked with coal and walk the halls of the inn every night in order to determine if the heat being generated was sufficient to ward off the effects of a cold winter's night. This chore was referred to as 'fire walking.' Hence, Harry was a 'fire walker.' "

Both Helen and Harry "absolutely loved the inn," Ron revealed. "They loved its location, its peacefulness and the huge pines that whistled as the constant wind blew through them from the lake." But one evening, as Harry was about to climb the staircase from the second floor to the third to perform his fire walker duties, he suffered a fatal heart attack.

By 1991, when Ron opened his business in the old Pinegrove Inn, he was familiar with the local legends claiming that Harry Corbett's essence never left the hotel after the man died. Ron had heard all the stories asserting that the previous owner's spirit "didn't want to go anywhere and remained at the inn, wandering in and out of the cabins on the property."

But no haunting could keep Ron from his business opportunity and he operated Pinegrove Inn as a bar-night-club in 1991. By that time, the third floor had been closed (or, more accurately, condemned) and the second floor was no longer used.

Harry Corbett's presence wasted no time in revealing itself to the new owner. "The very first day we opened, I remember pouring a scotch and water for a fellow," Ron wrote. "When I put the glass under the tap to fill it with water, the water would stop. As I took the glass away, the water started to pour. I put the glass back; the water stopped again." Perhaps realizing that he wasn't going to win this rather bizarre game, Ron took the glass to the nearby kitchen and filled it with the necessary amount of water from the kitchen tap without any trouble.

Ron continued relating stories of his paranormal encounters at the inn. "One cold January night at about midnight, I was at the bar. No one was in the building, and every door except the main entrance was bolted and locked," he wrote. Despite this, "I heard footsteps walking back and forth on the second floor. I thought to myself, *I'm hearing things and my mind is playing tricks on me.*"

But Ron wasn't even remotely convinced that all was well. "After gathering up a whole bunch of courage, I took a flashlight, because there was no power to the second floor, and slowly crept up the stairs to the spot where Harry had died. The sounds of the footsteps stopped. Everything appeared to be quite normal—until I pointed the flashlight at the hallway floor."

The sight that illuminated before Ron's eyes left him incredulous. "There were wet footprints coming out of the bathroom and continuing down the long hallway," he declared. "Absolutely no one was in that entire building except for me." What made the watermarks even stranger was that the water pipes that had once serviced the second floor had not been connected for more than two years.

Ron continued his tale. "Another evening—it was late, very late, around 4 AM—I went out to a shed that housed our walk-in cooler and beer storage to do a month-end inventory. For whatever reason, the lights in this shed never worked. We had two electricians look into it, but no one could find the problem, so we would just take out the trusty flashlight with us when we had to go out there."

On this particular night, Ron recalled that along with his flashlight he'd taken a clipboard, some pens, a beverage and the necessary keys out to the shed. What happened next still astounds him. "I was fumbling around trying to get the lock open when I suddenly lost everything I'd been carrying. My drink goes flying. Everything goes flying."

Not surprisingly, Ron's patience came to a quick end. "I lost it," he exclaimed. He shouted, "Harry, turn these lights on." The response was instantaneous. "BAMMM!!!!!!" the expressive man wrote. "It was as if someone was standing at the light switch and flicked it on. And these were the lights that had never worked."

Perhaps remembering his manners, or perhaps just trying to avoid any ghostly retaliation for his angry outburst, Ron immediately said, "Thank you, Harry."

Signs of the haunting continued. It became clear that if they were going to co-exist at the Inn, the man and the spirit would have to find a way to work together peacefully. Fortunately, the solution turned out to be a fairly simple one. "I determined that if I said 'Good morning, Harry,' and 'Good night, Harry,' the ghost was still mischievous but he minded his own business for the most part," Ron explained.

Ron Gostlin has gone on to other challenges by now, but I suspect that he misses his ethereal workmate, at least a little.

And I imagine that the ghost of Harry Corbett misses his interactions with Ron at the Pinegrove Inn they both loved so much.

The End